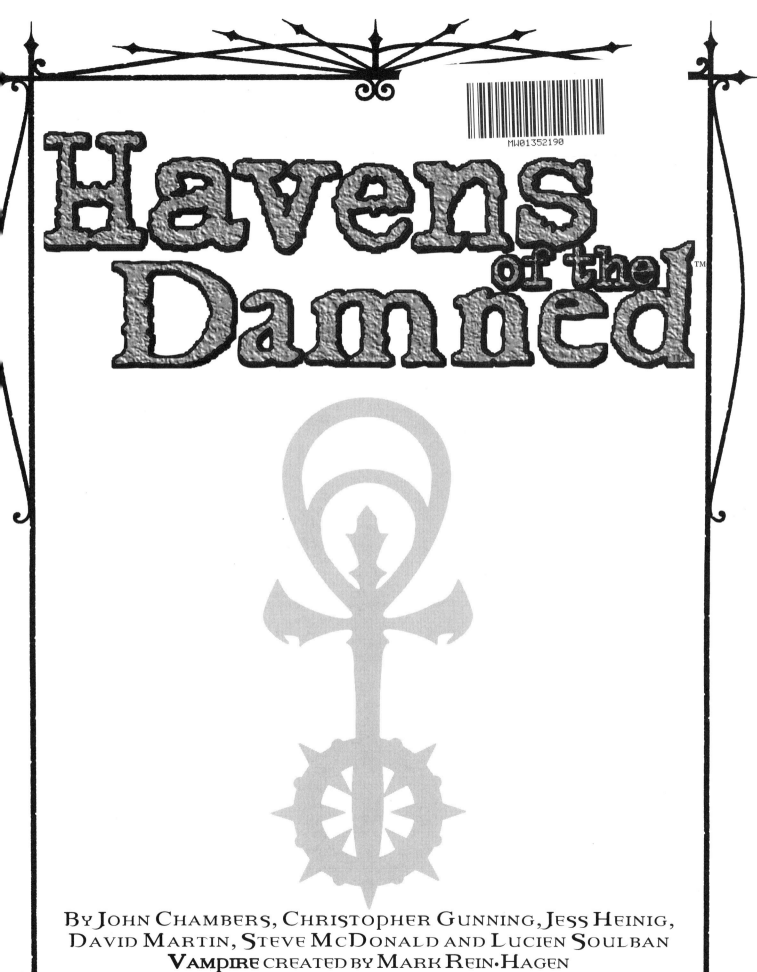

Havens of the Damned

By John Chambers, Christopher Gunning, Jess Heinig, David Martin, Steve McDonald and Lucien Soulban
Vampire created by Mark Rein•Hagen

Credits

Written by: John Chambers, Christopher Gunning, Jess Heinig, David Martin, Steve McDonald, Lucien Soulban. **Vampire** and the World of Darkness created by Mark Rein•Hagen.
Additional Material & Assistance: Shannon Hennessey, Jason Miller, Ed Spymoun
Developer: Carl Bowen
Storyteller Game System Design: Mark Rein•Hagen
Editor: Diane Piron-Gelman
Art Director: Richard Thomas
Layout & Typesetting: Pauline Benney
Interior Art: Michael Gaydos, Matt Mitchell, Jim Nelson
Front Cover Art: Jim Nelson
Front & Back Cover Design: Pauline Benney

Special Thanks

John "It's Done… I Guess" **Chambers** for giving it that ol' college try. And, yes, you *can* fight the Mist with "click-click."
Steve "She's the Future Wife of My Children" **McDonald** for that drunken Southern charm. And, yes, a Ka-Bar *is* a brilliant Christmas present.

735 Park North Blvd.
Suite 128
Clarkston, GA 30021
USA

© 2002 White Wolf Publishing, Inc. All rights reserved. Reproduction without the written permission of the publisher is expressly forbidden, except for the purposes of reviews, and for blank character sheets, which may be reproduced for personal use only. White Wolf, Vampire, Vampire the Masquerade, Vampire the Dark Ages, Mage the Ascension, Hunter the Reckoning, World of Darkness and Aberrant are registered trademarks of White Wolf Publishing, Inc. All rights reserved. Werewolf the Apocalypse, Wraith the Oblivion, Changeling the Dreaming, Werewolf the Wild West, Mage the Sorcerers Crusade, Wraith the Great War, Trinity and Havens of the Damned are trademarks of White Wolf Publishing, Inc. All rights reserved. All characters, names, places and text herein are copyrighted by White Wolf Publishing, Inc.

The mention of or reference to any company or product in these pages is not a challenge to the trademark or copyright concerned.

This book uses the supernatural for settings, characters and themes. All mystical and supernatural elements are fiction and intended for entertainment purposes only. This book contains mature content. Reader discretion is advised.

For a free White Wolf catalog call 1-800-454-WOLF.

Check out White Wolf online at
http://www.white-wolf.com; alt.games.whitewolf and rec.games.frp.storyteller
PRINTED IN THE UNITED STATES.

Havens of the Damned

Table of Contents

Introduction	4
The Winchester Mystery House	8
A Real Fixer-Upper	12
The Local	18
The Glass House	24
Downstairs Downtown	30
The House of Storms	36
The Guardian Lakes Country Club	42
The Elevator and the Arrow	48
Zatopek Farms	54
The Legend of Sensual Secrets	60
The Venetian	68
The Gatekeeper's Hold	74
The House that Fear Built	80
CVN 70 USS *Carl Vinson*	86
The Chattanooga Recreational Center	92

Introduction

Thou art my hiding place; thou shalt preserve me from trouble.
—Psalm 32, Verse 7

What Good is a Haven?

One of the things that many players take for granted when creating **Vampire** characters is their characters' haven. It's just an itty-bitty line at the top of the character sheet, but in the drama of the Kindred's unlives, it's where the Kindred rise and return every night. It's the sanctum of a Tremere, the estate of a Ventrue or Toreador, the drug den feeding pit of a Brujah or the laboratory of a Tzimisce.

The Kindred spend almost two thirds of their unlives in their havens. Perhaps not *exactly* that much, but unless a character is road-tripping, staying as a guest at someone else's haven or sleeping in the ground like a rabid Gangrel (which isn't really cost-effective in terms of nightly blood expenditure), he spends all of his daylight hours in one specific place.

Think, then, about what a Kindred wants from his haven. He's going to have to be in this place *forever*, or at least until the surrounding city structure changes so much that he needs to make according changes himself. It's where he goes to escape the sun and his enemies. It's where he goes to clear his mind and make ready to face one more night among his undead peers. It's the one place where he feels truly safe being himself. It's literally his shelter and safety against the ravages and vagaries of the Final Nights.

And yet, caught up in the drama and action of a **Vampire: The Masquerade** story, many players don't give a second thought to where their characters sleep. It's just somewhere the character goes once the session ends, and it's where he's on his way back from once the next session (and the next night of play) begins.

If developed and used with care, however, a character's haven can prove invaluable to the storytelling experience. It helps describe the character in ways he's not conscious of expressing. It can provide the character immediate access to the mundane equipment he needs to uphold the Masquerade or wage shadow wars against those who do. It can even serve as a pre-packaged setting for a scene, a session or an entire story. As much as the clothes he wears, the car he drives or the company he keeps, a Cainite's haven is an integral part of who he is.

What is a Good Haven?

That being said, what makes a Cainite's haven an effective part of a story as well as a necessity to a character's unlife? The specific details vary according to the haven's locale and the personality of the resident, but certain underlying facts remain constant. Regardless of its origin and nature, a character's haven is important for the safety it provides, the privacy it affords the inhabitant and its utility to the character (not to mention the Storyteller).

Safety

By the very definition of the word, a Cainite's haven must be a place of safety. It must keep out the deadly rays of the sun entirely, and it must be well fortified against the outbreak of fire. If the sunlight gets in or if a fire breaks out while the Kindred resident is sleeping, he or she might not wake up long enough to realize what has happened. If he does awaken, he might not remain lucid long enough to deal with the emergency in a rational, efficient manner. Rötschreck might just make him bug out and send him running into even more danger.

A Cainite's haven must also provide him safety from attack should his enemies try to do him harm while he sleeps or is simply hanging out at home. Should someone (whether a Lupine, a witch-hunter or just a greedy rival Cainite) discover the location of a vampire's haven, he must be able to keep that someone out or at least at bay long enough to make an escape or for help to arrive.

Privacy

Of course, one of the most effective safety features of a vampire's haven should be the fact that no one knows where it is. Even a haven that's part of a high-traffic public place ought to be tucked away in some area of it that no one would think to check. Most Cainites with more than a few years of unlife to their names know better than to share the locations of their havens with any of their fellow undead. One never knows, after all, whether a supposed friend will reveal himself to be an enemy as a result of a falling-out.

Aside from the safety issue, though, many Kindred have no desire to share the location of their havens anyway. Cainites are not only suspicious beasts, but selfish ones as well. They keep their most prized possessions at their havens, and sometimes the havens themselves are worthy of jealous vigilance. Any Kindred who lets others know that his haven (or something in it) is especially precious to him risks losing it to someone who wants it even more.

And, of course, concerns of the Masquerade cannot be ignored. A vampire must conceal his daytime resting-place, not only from his undead peers, but from the ignorant masses of humanity as well. The last thing any Cainite needs is for some mortal (or, God forbid, a gang of them) to come busting in on him while he's sleeping and unable to defend himself or otherwise deal with them.

Utility

The final factor that goes into making a good haven is what function it serves in a Kindred's unlife (if it serves one at all). Rather than just being a dark hole to sleep in, a haven can be the base of a Kindred's operations in undead society or even the site of some job for which mortals pay her.

Haven Creation

Creating a haven for a **Vampire** character isn't especially difficult. In fact, if you do so immediately after you create the actual character, while the ideas are still fresh in your mind, you shouldn't have much trouble at all. All you really need to do is think about the haven in stages, one by one, in the order you'd notice them if you were visiting the place.

The first thing you'd probably notice is what the haven looks like from the outside, so describe it and the community into which it fits. Where is this place geographically? What country, state, city, neighborhood and side of the street is it on? Now, what does it look like from the outside? Is it dark and foreboding? Is it tiny and pathetic? Does it blend in with the surrounding structures? Does it even look like a human structure? Have pains been taken to hide it, or does the character rely on the ignorance of his neighbors?

What you'd probably notice next is the security precautions. Is the place locked up with a row of dead-bolts on the door? Has the character set physical traps for the unwary? Is there some trick to getting inside, such as the doorknob being rigged to fall apart if it's turned to the right, thus barring entrance until the Kindred inside chooses to open it? Does the place have security cameras sweeping the scene or guard dogs on patrol? Once the place has been discovered, what means are in place to keep interlopers out?

Next, think about the interior of the haven. To the untrained mortal (or Cainite) eye, what kind of place is it? Is it a mundane building such as a bookshop or a hospital, in which the Kindred has hidden himself away? What does the place look like? How spacious is it? What sort of mood does being inside it evoke? If you look around, has the character left in the haven any clues to the fact that he's an undead drinker of blood? Building on that, what details about the place make it uniquely the Cainite character's own?

Finally, think about how the character uses his haven. Does he do some work there — which he can't do anywhere else — that is important to Kindred society somehow? To mortal society? Does he ever entertain Kindred guests there? If so, what provisions has he made for them? What about mortal guests? Does he lure victims back to his haven to feed, or must he work side by side with them there until it's time to sneak off to some secret niche and sleep away the sun?

New Background: Haven

As he did every night, Eric Parker, Beloved of Set, went through his ritual preparations. He placed the offering of a bowl of beer in the center of a ring of candles and sticks of sandalwood incense on the wood floor of his chamber. The lights were low. He began his silent prayers. All was in preparation....

The air conditioner rattling to life behind him interrupted his supplication. He rose rapidly and ran across the faded orange shag carpeting of his hotel room, hurrying to silence the thing before it was too late. As always, however, the machine refused to be quiet. It took a full minute to wind back down even after Eric forced its dial to the off position.

"Damnation!" he cried, then regretted his outburst a moment later at the usual angry thud from above of his upstairs neighbor's boot. "Sorry, sir," he said toward the ceiling, mentally adding his neighbor to the list of future slaves in his service.

First of all, keep in mind that the Haven Background is entirely optional. A player should not be forced to purchase this Background just to keep his character safe and hidden while the sun is up. The effects of certain other Backgrounds (such as Resources, Mentor, Fame and Status) can all include the character's access to a safe haven on any given day. A character with none of those other Backgrounds, however, can still have a perfectly reasonable haven as long as he has *this* Background. For instance, a character might not have enough money to afford a palatial mansion in today's economy, but if his great-grandmother left him one that had been fully paid for, there's no reason he can't remain in residence there.

The ratings of levels in this Background don't measure absolute values, but rather a scale of relative values. They might reflect how big your haven is or how important it is to mortal or Kindred society. (If such is the case, the rating will also show how desirable it is to other Kindred and how badly they'll want to take it for themselves.) By the same token, the rating might reflect how well hidden the haven is from seekers or how well defended against trespassers. This rating can also reflect how conveniently located the haven is to the local Rack and the most popular sites of Elysium.

• You stay in a seedy apartment in a dangerous and run-down section of town, or you're hiding among a great many people with whom you do not fit. The slightest slip and you'll be discovered.

•• You've upgraded to renting a decent apartment, a modest condo or small house. The neighborhood isn't great, but it's well clear of the Lupines' wilderness. People suspect that there's something funny about you, but they mind their own business for now.

••• You own the house you sleep in, or at least you never have to worry about making a house payment. The neighborhood is safe and kept up well. People have no reason to suspect that there's anything strange about you.

•••• You have either a very large house or a dilapidated mansion that no one else wants. There aren't many people around regularly, so you can feed in relative peace.

••••• Your haven is the equivalent of a well-maintained mansion. Feeding is easy most of the time, and remaining hidden and secure there isn't even in question. You'd have to actively try to let people find out about you here.

How to Use This Book

The remainder of this book is a random sampling of interesting or unusual havens of American Cainites from varied backgrounds, who use their havens in a variety of ways. The structure of each entry follows the same basic pattern. A brief description of the Kindred resident is followed by a quick explanation of how he or she came to dwell in the haven in question, as well as what makes it an important part of his or her nightly unlife. Next come descriptions of what the haven looks like, inside and out, and how it fits into the mortal and Kindred worlds. A good deal of that information focuses on how the resident ensures his safety and privacy while he's home, as well as any special concerns that feeding might raise in relation to the haven.

The last section of each haven write-up is a list of two to four quick story ideas. You can use and expand on these nuggets as inspiration for one-shot **Vampire** sessions, or you can slip them into an ongoing chronicle as your players' characters explore their Kindred society and get to know the other Kindred who make it up. You might even use one of them to start off an entirely new chronicle. If you're really up for a challenge, however, you can look for the subtle common threads that run through many of the suggested story ideas. If you can pick them out, you might want to construct a chronicle in which the characters have occasion to visit as many of the havens and interact with as many of the characters in this book as possible.

The Winchester Mystery House

In September 1862, at the height of the Civil War, Sarah Lockwood Pardee, talented musician and belle of the city, married William Wilt Winchester, sole heir to the Winchester Repeating Arms Company, in an elaborate ceremony in New Haven, Connecticut. In this perfect marriage of grace and wealth, the couple's wedded bliss seemed assured. Unfortunately, it was not to be.

Four years later, in July of 1866, the couple's first child, Annie, was born. What at first seemed a blessing would soon be marked by tragedy, however, as Annie contracted marasmus, a childhood wasting disease. To Sarah's horror, her Annie passed away soon after. Sarah was inconsolable, and she teetered for a time on the verge of madness. It took a decade for her to put her child's loss behind her and take the first tentative steps back into New Haven society life. Even still, the couple would never have another child.

Just as it seemed Sarah was getting her life back, her husband William was stricken with consumption, and he passed away in March of 1881. As his widow, Sarah inherited approximately $20 million and half ownership of the Winchester Repeating Arms Company. Wealth, however, did little to soothe Sarah's grief over the loss of her family.

Overwhelmed, Sarah took a friend's advice to visit a local medium in the hope of contacting the spirits of her lost husband and child. The medium fell into a trance and announced that the ghost of William Winchester was present and that he had a message for his widow. Speaking for Sarah's dearly departed, the medium told her that a curse had long since been laid on the Winchester family. The spirits of those whose lives had been cut short by the Winchester rifle could not rest easy, it seemed, and so they wished to have their revenge. Sarah learned that there was only one way she might appease these spirits. She must sell her home in New Haven and go west toward the setting sun. William's spirit would guide her to a new home for herself — and for the spirits that haunted her. Once she acquired her new domicile, she must then build upon it to house these lost souls. If construction ever halted, Sarah Winchester would die.

Taking the warning to heart, Sarah sold her New Haven home and headed west. She eventually came to California's Santa Clara Valley, where she found an eight-room farmhouse owned by a local doctor, Robert Caldwell. Something whispered to her that this was the site she had been looking for. Sarah purchased the farmhouse and the 162 acres of land on which it was situated, and thus began construction on what was to become the Winchester Mystery House.

For the next 38 years, work on the house never ceased. Day and night, the hammers fell and the saws whirred. Each night at midnight, Sarah would travel to the Séance Room in the heart of the house and glean from the spirits knowledge of what new details needed to be incorporated into the sprawling mansion. This cycle only ended in 1922, with Sarah Winchester's death.

That's the legend, anyhow. The truth is more complicated.

Resident

The Winchester mansion is more than a mere haven. It is also an elaborate trap designed to test its architect's theories about negative architecture and its effect on the human mind (and even the Cainite consciousness, to a lesser extent).

At the dawn of the 1800s, architect Jonathan Smith was eking out a modest existence designing public housing in Hartford, Connecticut. He might have made a better impression with his employers, though, had his designs been less needlessly elaborate and extravagant. Smith was an "artist" little concerned with practicality, which, given the structures he was designing, made him practically useless.

His designs did make an impression on one of Hartford's leading architects. Unfortunately, though, that architect was in no position to further Smith's career, as he was a centuries-dead Malkavian named Ivo Shandor. Impressed with Smith's clarity of vision — and with his reluctance to let little things such as practicality and function interfere with his view of how things should be — the vampire Embraced the young man, intent on molding him into a worthy heir to the ancient knowledge Shandor so valued.

Smith's transformation only intensified his obsession with his own unique architectural vision. For decades, he studied many of the dread secrets of occult architecture, learning from his sire how architects, carpenters and masons in times past created buildings according to principles of sacred geometry developed ages earlier by the peoples of Greece, Egypt and (as Shandor devoutly claimed) Atlantis. Intrigued, Smith began to incorporate these teachings into his own plans.

Yet, regardless of his keen interest, Jonathan Smith was a disappointment to Shandor. Smith's Embrace had robbed him of the very creative spark that had attracted his sire to him in the first place. Smith still possessed the same manic conviction in the infallibility of his designs, but his creativity had ossified, despite all the knowledge that his sire had imparted to him. As a result, real innovation seldom appeared in the plans that Smith drew up. Instead, his work was merely a hackneyed regurgitation of the ideas his sire expressed. He never seemed able to build on those ideas or express any genuinely creative impulse.

This state of affairs was intolerable to Shandor, who had hoped his childe's inventiveness would reinvigorate his own. Consumed by ennui, Shandor thought of ending his apprentice's unlife, followed by his own. In this, his darkest hour, the elder Cainite had an epiphany. Separately, each vampire was doomed never to know another moment of true creativity, but perhaps they could achieve greatness *together*. Shandor had heard tales of others of his clan who had successfully achieved a state of disembodied intelligence within the Malkavians' shared consciousness. Research on Shandor's part suggested that the state might be achieved through the Amaranth.

Therefore, in 1880, Jonathan Smith allowed himself to be talked into diablerizing his sire. Despite the fact that Shandor had wished, even planned, for this diablerie to occur, Hartford's prince called a blood hunt on the hapless neonate. Smith fled Hartford for his unlife, heading south to New Haven, where he had attended Yale University's School of Architecture.

While in New Haven, Smith learned (from the medium who had advised her) of Sarah Winchester's plan to move west with the intention of building a house as a repository for the spirits of those slain by the Winchester rifle. Taking as portents this information and the fact that he'd been driven out of Hartford to a town named New "Haven," Smith decided to follow the Winchester widow west. There, he would influence the construction of her new home to meet his own unique (read "insane") artistic sensibilities and truly test the merit of his sire's theory about reinvigorating the creative spark.

Each night at midnight, a bell would toll to summon the "spirits" to the Séance Room. Therein, hidden from view by his vampiric powers, Smith would direct the movement of the planchette that Sarah Winchester used to contact the "ghosts" that dwelled within her mansion. The unsuspecting woman believed that the messages Smith spelled out for her came from the spirits she was desperately trying to appease. Each morning, she would present the designs from the previous night's séance to the contractors in her employ.

Construction continued, day and night, for 38 years. Over that time, the whispering of Smith's sire within his mind grew to a shout, and the voice played on Smith's fear of Final Death to manipulate him. Shandor's voice explained to Smith that only within the house would he remain safe from the blood hunt called against him and that the two architects must work together to make of the house a labyrinth only they might fathom. More and more, Shandor's occult influence began to show through in the haven's construction. Mirrors were banned lest they accidentally misdirect the energies the house was meant to channel. The number 13, the sacred number of the clans and their Antediluvian founders, began to appear everywhere, from the number of palm trees on the lawn to the number of gas jets on the ballroom chandelier to the number of panes on certain windows — even to the number of bathrooms. Everything was constructed for purposes only the vampire who dwelled within could comprehend. Sometimes, even though the voice in his head assured him there was method to the madness, even Smith could not divine the reason behind his requests.

Over the years, the house continued to grow like a malignant cancer, engulfing several outlying structures in the process. Nevertheless, both Smith and the voice of his sire agreed that the work was finished as of September 4, 1922. To celebrate, Smith drank the widow Winchester dry. Sometimes, Smith hears her voice in his head, too. It's never as loud as Shandor's, though, so he seldom pays it any mind.

Since construction stopped, the paranoid Malkavian has remained within the house's grounds, trusting his blood-bound ghouls — first carpenters, later tour guides — to bring him suitable prey. The Mystery House is the only place where he feels safe.

Or at least he did until the Week of Nightmares. Shandor's voice has since "convinced" Smith that, with the rise of the Ravnos Antediluvian and the destruction of his kind, it's only a matter of time before the rest of the torpid Antediluvians stir from the fitful sleep of ages to fall upon their descendants. This prospect horrifies Smith more than the blood hunt ever did. In response, he has used a combination of arcane rituals and his own powers of Dementation to turn the mansion from a figurative representation of his tortured mind's madness to a literal one.

Appearance

The Winchester Mystery House sprawls across four acres of prime real estate in San Jose, an eye of maddening chaos in the very epicenter of the storm of rationality that is California's famed Silicon Valley. From the outside, the house looks like nothing more than an architectural curiosity, its myriad spider-web windows only hinting at the danger that lies at the haven's core. The house is largely Victorian in style, though on a much grander scale than others that were built during the period. Here and there, other architectural styles jut out from the edifice in sharp contrast to more uniform neighboring structures.

The grounds are finely landscaped and maintained, and are separated from the outside world by a six-foot-tall hedge whose only means of ingress is a large wrought-iron gate. Also located on the grounds of the Winchester House are the Winchester Historic Firearms Museum and the Winchester Products Museum.

Layout

The interior of the Mystery House is a confusing maze of rooms. It contains 950 doors, 52 skylights, 40 bedrooms, 13 bathrooms, six kitchens, two ballrooms, 40 staircases, 47 fireplaces and two basements. Many of these structures have little or no functionality. Several stairways lead only to blank ceilings, and all the stairways feature 13 steps except one, which has 42. This latter staircase only rises nine feet in a back-and-forth pattern (each of its steps is only two inches high). A child-size Toddler Balcony overlooks it. Several doors open onto blank walls. One room has a window in its floor. Some rooms were built within other rooms. The place is maddening enough, even before you add the house's Malkavian resident into the mix.

Nevertheless, such a creature is involved, and he has found a way to accentuate the mansion's negative effect on the minds of visitors. Between the midnight tolling of the house's bell and dawn, Smith tries to force his madness and the house into a sort of symbiosis. During this time, Smith believes that he can alter the structure of the house to suit his whims, making doors lead to rooms other than those they normally do, darkening windows to shut out light, and sealing all means of egress to the outside. Should some unfortunate soul be trapped inside the house, however, he actually becomes "only" the victim of Smith's mastery of the Dementation Discipline.

Three structures deserve special mention. In any of the house's various iterations, these structures remain firmly fixed in Smith's mind.

The Bell Tower

It is here that Jonathan Smith performs his nightly blood ritual, tolling the bell at midnight while sacrificing a portion of his vitae to tie his fractured mind to the equally fractured structure of the house he designed.

The Séance Room (The Blue Room)

This room is the only one in the house that Smith feels is beyond his mental reach, although he offers no reason why this might be so. Characters finding themselves here who attempt to use the planchette located on the table in the room's center might be able to converse with the spirit of Sarah Winchester, who will do whatever she can to convince them to destroy the monster who killed her. If the characters agree to do so, she will give them whatever information she has to aid them.

The Door to Nowhere

Most of the time, this door leads only to a two-story drop into the garden. However, between midnight and dawn, it leads… somewhere else. Since no one has ever come back, it is difficult to ascertain exactly where that might be. The doorway may reach across the Shroud to deposit those who are unfortunate enough to pass through it into the Underworld. It may also somehow lead into the deep recesses of Jonathan Smith's mind. Nobody, except possibly Smith himself, knows for sure, and he's terrified of going through the door himself.

Story Ideas

• Working at the behest of their prince and an obsessive archon who's in town from the East Coast, the players' characters' coterie is enlisted to help track down "an escaped diablerist with ties to the infernal" who has apparently taken up residence in Santa Clara. When they put together what clues the archon has about where his quarry might have gone, however, they realize that he's actually looking for Jonathan Smith. If they aren't inclined to believe Smith capable of what he's being accused of, they visit him at the Mystery House and learn his account of his past. The coterie must then decide if the archon's claims are exaggerations or outright lies and what to do about Smith once the archon finds out that the characters know where he is.

• A pack of Sabbat Inquisitors investigates the Winchester Mystery House on a tip from a local informant and discovers that there is more to Jonathan Smith's (and, by extension, his sire's) theories of sacred geometry than either Malkavian knew. The Inquisitors can deduce that, through a bizarre confluence of astrological alignments, numerological coincidences and other bad luck, Jonathan Smith has managed to trap a demonic spirit somewhere in his haven. The Inquisitors must get into the house, find out where the spirit is trapped and banish the thing, all while dealing with Smith's own Dementation-based defenses (and possibly a crazed and desperate Smith himself).

• An enterprising land developer begins greasing palms and making deals in the area to buy the land on which the Winchester Mystery House and the two Winchester museums are located, hoping to develop them into something that will make the city more money. He has made arrangements to relocate the museums to nearby smaller cities (thereby hopefully boosting those cities' economies as well), and he intends to level the eyesore that the Mystery House has grown into. He's even made some progress convincing the local historical preservation society to let him do the latter. In light of this distressing news, Jonathan Smith comes to the coterie for help. He needs the characters to use what influence they can on his behalf, and he tells them to name their price. Once they've given their word and started doing as Smith asks, however, they discover that the land developer is the pawn of a powerful elder Kindred whom even their sires and/or mentors are afraid to challenge.

A Real Fixer-Upper

Vampires all over the world have one thing in common: they were all, at one time, inexperienced childer searching for a place that they could call their own. Not all of these childer come from sires who are already loaded down with wealth and social status, and not every elder can (or chooses to) supply his newly created progeny with the essentials to survive as they learn their place in this world. Those without such support are left to fend for themselves, but many emerge stronger than their better-supported peers do. The Setite childe known as Eric Parker is a case in point.

Resident

Eric Parker was a casino dealer in his mortal life, with an uncanny ability to keep the most destitute and unlucky people at the tables, even when they knew they were in over their heads. The house prospered at their expense, and Eric lived very well as a result. He dressed in sharp, stylish clothes, lived in a fancy condo on the edge of town and drove a restored convertible Camaro. He dated exotic dancers from the high-quality establishments downtown, and when he got tired of them, he traded up for someone at a different club. As he saw things, it was all thanks to suckers who didn't know when to call it quits.

In fact, Eric lived so well, and with so little regard for those who blew their savings trying to hit it big, that he caught the eye of a Setite who happened to use the place as a meeting point for his mortal contacts. The Setite saw in Eric a willful charmer of and (predator upon) those of inconstant resolve. One such as Eric, the Setite decided, could be a valuable and powerful acolyte in Set's service.

Unfortunately for Eric, his sire felt that struggle best helps focus the young mind and thus breeds the best servants for Set. As a result, the first four months in which Eric has served his new god have been the hardest months of his existence. In the first three months after his selection, his master forced him through a series of rigorous tribulations, each designed to remove the blinders placed upon him by the world Set's enemies created. The first of these tests involved the destruction of Eric's mortal life and the things that made that life comfortable. His master took away his car, his apartment, his job, his finances and even saw to it that his regular lady friends were offered better-paying, irresistible jobs in different cities. Eric awoke one night to find everything gone and a clipping from a local newspaper with his own obituary in it. "Nothing of the old life can remain, except for you," his master had written on the clipping, "and it shall be the final test of faith for you to bring yourself up again."

At the conclusion of this first stage of instruction, Eric relocated to the Atlantic City area with nothing but the clothes on his back. Initially, he slept in whatever covered spaces he could occupy before dawn. He landed in Dumpsters, abandoned buildings, junk cars or any other place that could keep out the deadly sun and hide him from prying mortals. Yet, even during this time, Eric was looking for a way to move up. Although Eric's sire undoubtedly would have been disappointed with Eric's unoriginal ideas, his bestial urges and his idealized impression of his sire as a gracefully subtle tempter inspired him to try to find a place in the world of crime.

The local scene was unpromising, however, and crowded besides. It seemed to Eric that all of the areas of vice for which the younger members of his clan were supposedly known had already been sewn up by other factions. And those factions, he unfortunately discovered, were not of a mind to share. Therefore, Eric fell back (temporarily, he kept telling himself) on his mortal skills and returned to the casino lifestyle. Trying to play it cool, lest he give his sire the impression that he's somehow cheating, he turns in a workmanlike performance at night behind a blackjack table, and with the money from this new position, he has finally arranged a modest shelter for himself. He now occupies a room on the basement floor of the Traveler Rest hotel, three blocks east of his place of employment.

Appearance

The Traveler Rest is one of a string of cheap, nightly-rate motels scattered down the roadway three blocks east of the entertainment district. The various establishments (mainly bars and "gentlemen's clubs," as well as the occasional liquor store) are often the last refuge for those who can no longer keep up with the high-roller lifestyle in the heart of the city. The mien of the crowd functions as a timeline of urban decay, with old people in dated fashions weaving in and out of streets that have long since been given over to vice. Streams of terminally trendy young people move in and out of alleys as well, plying some of the world's most ancient trades here, rather than allowing their own streets to be sullied. The Traveler Rest's neighborhood is a cavalcade of dirty people appearing in styles that would make a Mafia wife wince, and engaging in practices (such as drug-dealing, prostitution, robbery and worse) that shame all but the most jaded few.

From the outside, it's hard to distinguish the Traveler Rest from the surrounding buildings. It is a three-story walkup, with little more to advertise its existence than a buzzing, flickering, Eisenhower-era neon sign on the front that currently reads " O EL-CH AP RAT S" and is in danger of losing several more vowels. The exterior still sports its original paint job, although what the color actually was is now a matter for some debate. The place was originally intended to attract vacationers and businessmen, but the current clientele largely comprises prostitutes and johns, drug dealers and their customers, and those who are simply too poor or addled to seek better accommodations.

Layout

Considering the state of the outside of the building and the condition of the surrounding neighborhood, the hotel's seedy interior comes as no great surprise. As a customer enters what passes for a lobby in this part of town, a disgruntled and perpetually sweating night clerk regards him from within a steel cage, a look of disdain on his jowls. A black-and-white 13" television (whose reception is intermittent at best) squats underneath a hand-lettered sign that reads, "Ask About Our Sheet Rental." Low rent is the theme here, and rates start from $10 an hour to $40 a week. About half of the rooms are full on any given night, and the majority of the occupants are paying some variation of the hour rate. Eric is an oddity in that regard, which is something he will strive to cover up once he becomes experienced enough to recognize it as a flaw.

The hallways are covered in carpets worn by 50 years of foot traffic to a patchwork of gray shading, and the rooms themselves are individual monuments to poor upkeep. Most of the doors are discolored and perpetually sticking in their frames as a result of water damage from a crack-pipe-ignited fire three years ago. Should a visitor manage to work the door open, he enters a shag-carpeted throwback furnished with a dilapidated bed (or two, depending on what the renter desires) and illuminated by a swag lamp that hangs from the ceiling. A (once) white-tiled bathroom with a narrow shower stall is on the immediate right of the door, with a fine collection of molds, spores and mildew forming a surreal homage to Vincent van Gogh on the shower curtain. Old pre-fabricated vinyl furniture dominates the remainder of the bed area, with chintzy faux African woodcuts on the wall and a wheeled metal cart that sports a clone of the lobby television. The reception in most of the rooms is better than that downstairs, but HBO is definitely not an option.

Eric's Haven

Eric's particular room is on the ground floor next to the janitorial closet. The space was used to store what furniture had finally crossed the line into being deemed unserviceable (usually by collapsing while a guest was using it) before Eric arrived, but he managed to make it his own in short order. The young Setite is particularly proud of this accomplishment, as it was his first successful attempt to bend a mortal to his will. Granted, the masterful manipulation that he employs involves sneaking a bottle of whisky back from the casino now and again for the desk clerk, but a success is a success regardless. This particular room is well secured against sunlight, as the only window was long ago covered in sheet metal after the previous manager caught a gang of runaways trying to break in and use the empty room as a flophouse. Since he moved in, Eric has added a rubber gasket to the bottom of the door to further block any unwanted light.

Despite the decidedly seedy accommodations, Eric is doing his best to turn his poor excuse for a haven into a proper home for one of his faith. Given his lack of funds, however, he has to do it on the cheap. He makes ritual offerings of beer, which comes from six packs bought at the corner gas station, and he takes the bus to the suburbs once a month in order to buy incense and candles at a cut-rate arts and crafts store out at the mall.

On weeks when tips are heavy and his personal gambling goes well, Eric occasionally splurges at the Discovery Channel Store located at the outlet mall, picking up Egyptian-style knickknacks to add to his home. Items he's already purchased include a small throw rug with a scene from the Egyptian Book of the Dead woven into the fibers, an ink pen set with the utensils styled in the image of Set and Sekhmet and a Dover edition of *Egyptian Magic and Ritual* by E.A. Wallis Budge.

Eric is extremely self-conscious about his lackluster attempts to propitiate his god. He has begun to scout the surrounding area for potentially useful mortal supplicants to his faith, but he does not feel powerful enough to begin active "preaching" in the near term. He also doesn't want to embarrass his sire by spreading the word before he's truly ready (thus making himself look like a fool and sullying Set's image). Given the poverty and moral bankruptcy of his surroundings, however, the Traveler Rest would make an ideal center for worship once he has garnered sufficient knowledge and strength to warrant a following.

Security

The watchword for Eric's attempts to protect himself and his haven is paranoia. His feeding practices still show the same caution and discretion as when he was slumming it in alleyways. Animals are his primary targets, while passed-out drunks and addicts make for an occasional gourmet meal. He varies his route to and from work as best he can (although there are only a small number of variations for so short a distance), and he studiously avoids any use of his supernatural abilities within a block of the casino. This practice unwittingly fulfills the desires of his sire, as Eric is forced to use his innate cunning and persuasive abilities to get what he wants from the people

around him, rather than unnatural powers that he may never fully master.

In his haven, Eric is striving to be the best tenant in the history of the Traveler Rest. Those few tenants who have met and recognize him remember him as that quiet, polite young man downstairs. He is fastidiously clean, and he always disposes of any mess that his primitive attempts at worship may leave in the room. Doing so has been easy up to this point, since he doesn't have the confidence in his own faith necessary to arrange a large-scale ceremony (and thus potentially make a large-scale mess). In fact, the only thing that might seem odd to anyone searching the room (other than the tenant's obsession with cleanliness in such a dive) would be the lack of a Gideon's Bible. The room used to have one — the inside covers of which were filled with the pager numbers of pimps and two-bit drug-dealers — but Eric has long since used its pages in one of his earliest attempts at a ritual. He keeps the empty card-stock cover in the drawer of his nightstand, though, out of a sense of personal irony.

Eric is not currently familiar with the full scope of Kindred society in Atlantic City, and he hopes things will stay that way. Consequently, he is also unaware that the relatively low number of Kindred in the city to begin with aids his effort at remaining hidden. Prior to the fall of the Sabbat stronghold in New York, Atlantic City did have a significant vampiric population, mostly Camarilla. Now that they have achieved their objective (i.e., "reclaiming" New York), the former Camarilla residents have left their Atlantic City operations in the hands of mortal and ghoul functionaries. Therefore, Eric is currently beneath the notice of the majority of Camarilla agents, as his dime-store bank account doesn't fit the stereotypical image most have of a Follower of Set.

Locating the Unexceptional

Despite his low beginning, Eric is valuable for his potential. A Setite entering a power vacuum, even one as inexperienced as Eric, is a dangerous thing. If he manages himself correctly, he could become a powerful figure in Atlantic City in as little as a decade. Should more Cainites move into the area unaware of his presence, the difficulty in locating Eric stems from that of discerning any change in broader society that would indicate Eric's presence. His actions do little to disturb the surrounding community, so only the most perceptive searchers would be able to find evidence that he's around (provided they were looking to begin with).

In fact, most of those who seek Eric will do so only if he makes some error that indicates a dangerous vampire is in the neighborhood. It is entirely possible that some major loss (such as a bad night of after-work gambling, for example) could put Eric in a sour enough state of mind to unleash his darker half and send him out into the night to cause some actual trouble. Eric's unlife is so small-time, though, that even the most talented investigators would still have difficulty locating him afterward.

It is also possible that mortal relations of Kindred in the area may fall victim to Eric's prodding at the blackjack tables. The signs of his influence are barely distinguishable from normal gambling addiction, however, and should Eric discover any sort of connection between the local vampire community and a particular gambler, he will do his best to avoid that mortal from that point on. He would even be willing to have that customer banned from the casino altogether, if he can convince his manager to do so.

Should he foul up a night's hunting or accidentally step on some powerful elder vampire's toes, Eric's current escape plan is meager, as befits his resources. Should cash be an absolute requirement, he plans on removing the cash box from his blackjack table and obfuscating himself while crouching down out of sight. He'll then use the funds to purchase a bus ticket to take him as far as the approach of the sun will allow. Eric is unaware that his schooling in the Discipline is insufficient to hide him from cameras or Cainites with supernatural powers of perception, but he intends to be well on his way out of town, courtesy of Greyhound, before anyone knows he's gone for good.

Story Ideas

• In order to test his progeny's wits and survival instinct, Eric's sire convinces a coterie of characters who owe him a favor to help him out. He has them find Eric's room at the Traveler Rest and await Eric there until about an hour before dawn. At that point, they're to surprise Eric, attack him and try to stake him without killing him, all before sunup. If they can, they're to return Eric to his sire for more intensive instruction. There's no harm done if they can't catch him, of course, because that will mean that Eric is progressing as well as his sire had hoped.

• At some point in the future, Eric makes a move to "take control" of the casino at which he works. His methods involve a blood bond, blackmail and coercion of the rightful owner, but he doesn't realize that said owner is already the pawn of a more powerful vampire who has moved on to live in New York City. Annoyed (and not a little insulted) by Eric's rough treatment of his lackey, the older Kindred sends a group of his agents (i.e., the players' characters) to find Eric, track him back to his haven and teach him a lesson. After that, they're instructed to try to recruit Eric as one of their own so that their employer can keep better track of him in the future.

- Two prostitutes and their respective customers at the Traveler Rest are making so much noise one morning as Eric returns home from a bad night at the casino that he can't immediately drop off to sleep. Sticking close to the walls and well away from any distant windows, he makes his way to their adjoining rooms and screams at them to keep it down or else. The unusual outburst gets the attention of his neighbors and even the desk clerk, but the noise stops. That night, however, Eric is woken up by policemen breaking into his room and arresting him for murder. Someone, it seems killed the four people he was seen screaming at, and he was named as the likely suspect because of his outburst. Desperate, he calls his master, who calls on the only vampires he knows of in the Atlantic City area (i.e., some of the players' characters). In return for a boon, Eric's master asks them to get Eric out of jail before sunrise and either help him figure out what actually happened or get him out of town in secret if he's actually guilty.

The Local

Wars, especially long ones, tend to form strong bonds of loyalty and reliance between those who go through them together. Counting on one another for backup when everyone's lives (or unlives) are on the line breeds a familiarity and trust among comrades in arms that is nearly impossible to break. The same is especially true when those comrades' jobs involve stealth, secrecy, deep-cover work and operations behind enemy lines. Such soldiers must be able to work, relax, get along and even live with one another, because when it comes down to it, no one else can be said to have their best interests so firmly in mind.

If you throw an unending sect conflict between undying soldiers into the mix and add the mystical group blood bond of the Vaulderie as well, the strength of that bond can't help but intensify. That being the case, the vampires who rely on each other the most can't help but make their havens together regardless of the nature of the quarters they choose. In these, the Final Nights, solidarity is the key to victory.

Residents

The pack of Sabbat Cainites known as the Sparticists has made a name for itself in pre-siege intelligence gathering. Its discovery of key information on Camarilla weaknesses led to the initial assault on the former Camarilla stronghold of Detroit, and the protection it provided the city from a counterattack of Camarilla-driven influence shortly thereafter helped new Sabbat residents establish an unshakable hold on the city. The pack has been developing its methods for some time, as the pack's founders have been of the blood and working together since the First World War.

Matthais Kohler, ductus of the Sparticists, was a member of the German political movement of the same name. Essentially socialist, the movement's political philosophies instilled in Kohler a deep-seated hatred of entrenched interests. In the post-war period, the civil unrest that accompanied the fall of the government wedded his political philosophies with the knowledge of how to survive in a period of struggle. This learning experience attracted the interest of the European Sabbat, which arranged his recruitment. Since that time, the pack that took him in has done well for itself, using a highly cautious approach to operations in order to succeed where more visible packs would fail.

When entering a new target area, and in keeping with Kohler's collectivist roots, the method of infiltration favored by the Sparticists involves placing a trusted aide (currently their pawn Grimaldi) in a position of authority within a politically active non-profit organization. Such organizations are often unknowingly opposed to Camarilla pawns in the area (given many Camarilla elders' interest in businesses and governmental affairs) by the very nature of their work, and their employees and volunteers are easy to motivate to perform actions "for the cause" that, in fact, benefit their puppet-masters.

With the pack priest and two other members staying just outside the city to support the mission and to provide backup in case of emergencies, Kohler and the remainder of the Sparticists moved into the area approximately one year ago. They selected Local Office 1111 of the State Janitorial and Maintenance Workers Union as a base of operations for a variety of reasons, foremost among which is the poverty of its members.

The economic outlook of the city of New Orleans, where Local 1111 is located, is schizoid in the extreme. The tourist districts abound with a colorful entertainment and gambling community, and music and good times are available 24 hours a day. The vast majority of the city's residents will never see it, though, as the wages offered by those same industries provide for precious little save the essentials. As might be expected in a city founded on fast living, the city government is famously corrupt. The individual citizen can find no satisfaction and very few solutions.

The janitors of the Local still face difficult economic straits, despite the benefits they gain by organizing. As a consequence, many of them are quite willing to assist their union in whatever way they can, as long as doing so results in tangible rewards for them. This culture of activism is the key to the Sparticists' stratagem. The members are joined by a common goal: to improve their lot in life by collective action. As Kohler knew from his mortal years, the harmony of purpose created by such a common ideal creates a very motivated set of tools. When an enlightened master utilizes these tools, they go a long way toward countering the Camarilla edge in raw monetary resources.

More importantly, from Kohler's view, is the membership's access to city institutions. The members of Local 1111 have won assignments throughout the city, and the nature of their jobs requires that they be given access to nearly all areas of the buildings that they must enter, ranging from government offices to the suites of financial institutions.

Before the arrival of Kohler and his packmates, Local 1111 was one of the most active unions in the city, with a proven track record of social change. Its members worked hard to build a strong union, one through which they could work to improve their lives by helping each other. The members of Local 1111 love the organization they created as a result of their own labor, an organization that fights for good purposes in their names. Visitors could often find members of the Local coming over after their regular janitorial assignments in order to help clean up the office.

When Kohler decided that Local 1111 would become a tool for his mission, however, he began the slow strangulation of the good of Local 1111. Initial contact came through Kohler's servitor, Esteban Grimaldi. Grimaldi is the latest in a series of ghouls whom the Sparticists use, since he's sufficiently human to interact with untainted mortals during daylight hours on behalf of the pack. He serves as the new Executive Director, hired to handle the Local's day-to-day operations on behalf of the elected officers. He got this job through one of the side effects of his years as a front man for the Sparticists — an extensive résumé with many similar positions at other non-profit organizations.

Shortly after being hired and put in place, Grimaldi initiated the inevitable ruin of the Local by pulling money out of activism and simply making shady deals with the right politicians in order to keep the membership happy. The money is being diverted into a deceptively titled "Rebirth" fund, the supposed purpose of which is, in Grimaldi's words, to "take [the Local] to the next level of activity in the city."

The truth of the matter, though, is twofold. Union dues are being used to arrange hiding places for the Sabbat packs that will arrive in the next wave of operations once the Sparticists have completed their intelligence-gathering objectives. These hiding places consist mainly of derelict buildings in the worst parts of town, and the cover for their purchase is in the form of money funneled to a "Community Redevelopment Fund" that Grimaldi set up in cooperation with the city. The New Orleans city government is happy for the cash, of course, so it's in no hurry to discover any secrets that its new business partner may be hiding.

The money with which Grimaldi is playing his shell game also assists the Sparticists in keeping their presence hidden while they perform their tasks. The money in and of itself doesn't hide them, obviously, but the liquidity it gives to their operations makes implementing their plan much easier than it would be on a budget.

Appearance

The offices of Local 1111 are ramshackle in the extreme, since many of the repairs on the structure have been performed by members of the Local in order to save much-needed dues money for other tasks, such as political action and organizing of non-union janitors in the area. Local 1111 has taken up residence in a former funeral home, which was itself a two-story former townhouse donated by a now-defunct urban renewal project. The avenue on which the street rests is well planned but not well maintained. Cracks web the surface concrete, and several severe potholes pock the surface as well. Large oak trees line the sides of the avenue, providing some relief from the stifling summer heat for those who take the bus or must park across the street.

A set of wide marble steps rises up out of the sidewalk and grafts onto the building's porch. By night, the steps serve as a combination bedroom and bathroom for the local derelicts, and the marble is the worse for wear because of it. To the left of the stairs, a small carport with a corrugated aluminum awning leads off of the road. Grimaldi's white, seven-year-old Ford Taurus can be found in the carport during business hours. All other visitors and staff park at the 24-hour grocery store across the street.

Layout

Inside, the above-ground floors of Local 1111 are fairly normal for a non-profit organization. Visitors there find patched-together furniture, computers ranging in age from one decrepit Macintosh Classic II to a trio of Packard Bell PCs with the words "Designed for Windows 95!" proudly emblazoned on their dingy shells. Stacks of motivational literature abound on the office's many metal bookcases as well. Their content is generic, which makes them significant and useful to anyone with a background in the labor movement. The literature is essentially about what the Local has *done*, not what it *plans to do*. These exercises in generic writing share bookshelf space with such labor classics as *Confessions of a Union Buster* and *The AFL-CIO's Guide to Labor Organizing*.

Framed photographs of union activities and former members adorn every wall, including a series of head shots of the former Presidents and Executive Directors of the place. (One oddity about this series of pictures is the fact that Mr. Grimaldi's space is still blank.) The foyer opens onto a cluster of tan-walled cubicles, with one large office (occupied by Grimaldi) off to the side. The cubicles are festooned with posters and noteworthy newspaper clippings, on which left-wing political stances are a common theme. Although Grimaldi has begun to discourage it (to minimize "accidents" involving his masters), members or staffers can often be found working here late into the evening.

Grimaldi's offices are similar to those inhabited by the other staffers, but perceptive or artistically inclined viewers may note that Grimaldi seems to be going through the motions when it comes to his decorations. Further, none of the notable objects he displays seem to name him or refer to him specifically. His trophies and plaques all proudly proclaim some objective met by a non-profit he has been associated with in the past, but his name in never listed in the words engraved on them. This seems to go for almost everything in his office, and just as in the foyer area, all the pictures on his walls lack his image.

The most obvious signs of the Sparticists' presence appear in the basement, so Grimaldi has taken great pains to secure that area. One of the first purchases the union made under his direction was a security system for the building, dividing the building into two zones and requiring an employee to key in a four-digit code number on a small panel at the entrance to each one. The upper area of the basement is the first such zone, and staffers know the alarm's code for it. Only Grimaldi and the Sparticists know the second basement zone's code. In addition, the door is locked by a regular deadbolt to which Grimaldi possesses the only key.

The door to the basement is located at the rear of Grimaldi's office. Behind that door, a set of stairs leads down into an uninteresting room with a dirt floor. A single 40-watt bulb dangling from a chain illuminates this space. Boxes of bric-a-brac are located here on handmade shelves, as are signs from long-ago picket lines, literature endorsing candidates from past electoral campaigns and buttons emblazoned with "Impeach Nixon Now!" and "Labor for McGovern-Shriver '72." Grimaldi has had any items that his ignorant human employees are likely to need (such as spare office equipment or recent files) moved upstairs long ago, so no member of the staff has had any reason to go downstairs in quite some time.

To the right of the stairs is a set of double doors marked "Records Storage," which is double-locked from the outside. Grimaldi possesses one of two keys to these doors, and Kohler keeps the other on his person at all times. The locks can be opened from the inside, of course, with a simple click of a latch. The reason for this room's importance is Grimaldi's insistence on redundancy of files. He has required copies of all documentation, no matter how seemingly insignificant, to be kept here.

The interior of this room is also the heart of the nascent Sabbat operation in the city, serving as a combination command center and a crash pad for Grimaldi's sleeping masters. The room itself widens out from the door, going back about 30 feet under the floorboards of the Local. A pair of tables has been put together in the center of the room, and maps and various photocopied reports from unwitting agents are strewn across them. A row of cots is arrayed around the area as well, and anyone who manages to enter this room while the pack is away will note that the inhabitants are strictly roughing it. Near Kohler's cot, a small pile of candles has been placed and… something has recently been ripped apart there, judging by the dried blood on the floor and the thin shriveled strips half-buried in the dirt beneath. Other personal touches in the area include a small tie tack with the legend "Friend of the Abraham Lincoln Brigade" on it.

In addition, a variety of small furniture items have been smuggled into the room. Two small bookshelves stand against the far wall, containing a selection of titles that ranges from *The Gunsmith's Bible* to Voltaire's *Candide* in a German translation. A workbench with a lamp mounted on it has a selection of tools hanging from the wall behind it, and small metal parts are arranged on the bench itself. A character with a working knowledge of firearms (i.e., with a successful Intelligence + Firearms roll) may recognize slightly modified parts of various commercially available small arms. Metal slivers on the bench and in the dirt floor suggest that someone's been filing off serial numbers, and discarded firing pins show signs of reduction, possibly in an attempt to increase the firing rate of legal firearms.

Security

Having been undertaking undercover stealth missions for decades, the Sparticists know that the best form of security in enemy territory is anonymity. Through their tool Grimaldi, they have altered the operations of the Local to avoid attracting the attention of prying mortal eyes (in hopes of likewise avoiding Camarilla Kindred scrutiny thereby). As a result, the Local has shut down much of its visible political operations, concentrating instead on behind-the-scenes deal-making that sacrifices the long-term health of the Local in exchange for short-term gains designed to keep the members happy. These deals buy small contractual gains for the membership at the expense of greater freedoms, such as letting slide contract clauses with employers that prevent the union from striking. Other arrangements involve a dramatic drop in activism. This change in strategy has resulted in Local 1111 dropping out of the public eye, which in turn allows the Sparticists greater freedom of action.

Another level of security offered by this haven is the Local's own members, whose existence allows the Sparticists to perform most of their intelligence gathering through a blind layer of unwitting pawns. Those pawns make themselves available through the office membership rolls, which is the reason the Sparticists chose it. The pack gathers information on a particular business in a Camarilla city by having Grimaldi send organizers to non-union workplaces (ones that are likely rooks on some Kindred chessboard) and try to pinpoint the site's most discontent employees. The Sparticists then instruct Grimaldi to make contact with said employees and offer them ways to "get even" with their employers in exchange for supporting the Local's organizing efforts.

If a suspected Camarilla-influenced workplace already patronizes union janitors and maintenance people, Grimaldi and the Sparticists use basically the same approach. They scan the Local's membership rolls and match the names there with those of people who've filed large numbers of complaints against the target employer or who seem to need a little help paying their union dues on time. They then make deals with the most suitable union workers to have them bring back important information.

In addition, the unwitting agents of the pack have been instructed to avoid any action at their job sites that would draw attention to themselves or the surveillance they are undertaking. They ask their agents to copy documents rather than steal them, and even then only if the information therein is so complex or crucial that a simple summary just won't do. The members have been told that current "valuables" to look out for include any documentation that contains financial information or is directed to the supervisors of whichever establishment the particular janitor is active in. The goal of the current stage of the campaign is to flush out signs of Camarilla influence over important businesses in the city, and to try to identify agents of its intelligence network.

Discovery

The Sparticists are a very skilled pack, and discovering them will not be an easy thing to accomplish. It is more likely that those persons concerned with Camarilla security in the city will become aware of the shift in funds at Local 1111, especially if the searcher has influence in the mortal laboring community. Possible clues include the ending of a long-term activist relationship between Local 1111 and any of the other non-profit organizations with which it associates. Local 1111 has a long history of this sort of cooperation, so almost any type of public organization could be the other half of such a relationship.

Unfortunately for an investigator, the shift in priorities evidenced by Local 1111 is not necessarily unusual. Those seeking the Sparticists would likely have to hear more than reports that a union is falling down on the job to realize that something fishy is going on. A more obvious warning sign would be a botched "favor" on the part of one of the janitors. Should he be arrested for breaking into an employer's office at Grimaldi's request, his story might raise some intense local interest. Through Grimaldi, the union would deny all responsibility, but such a story would make interesting reading for any mortal investigators with Camarilla masters to serve.

Another possibility comes in the form of prior experience. Should a current member of the Camarilla be a former resident of a city that the Sparticists have previously targeted, then the subtle signals put out by Local 1111's actions could be sufficient to jog old (and painful) memories.

There is always the chance, however, that the Sparticists may make a move more visible than normal. Half the pack is outside the city, and circumstances may force Kohler's people to travel outside the city in order to regroup. Kohler would want to put off doing so for as long as possible, but developing troubles in a previously conquered city or the requirements of the Sabbat "faith" (as acted out by the *ritae*) may require a reunion.

Story Ideas

• A pack of elders within the Sabbat have decided that now is the time for the Sword of Caine to establish its dominance in the city of New Orleans. They're preparing a wave of violent attacks and upheavals designed to shock the established Camarilla Kindred into all-out retreat, but first they must find out where these Kindred are and what influence they have over the city. Therefore, a specialized pack known as the Sparticists (i.e., the players' characters) must sneak into the city and gather intelligence of importance to the soldiers massing for the assault. An opportunity exists to insinuate itself within the offices of Local 1111,

but the pack must operate very carefully. In the aftermath of Sabbat attacks up and down the East Coast, the influx of bizarre Cathayans on the West Coast, and even unimaginable terrorist attacks by mere mortals, the Camarilla Kindred in the city have grown especially vigilant and paranoid where security is concerned.

• It may just be paranoia, but the characters' Camarilla elders are convinced that an all-out Sabbat invasion of their city is imminent. For weeks, the elders have had the players' characters haring all over New Orleans investigating the slightest oddity in the way their city runs itself, and tonight is no different. It seems a union janitor was caught breaking into the locked office of a manager of a bank where a local Ventrue keeps a safe-deposit box. Investigating him probably won't turn up anything, but it never hurts (or pisses off one's elders) to be thorough….

• A mere week before an invasion of New Orleans by a pack of elders is to begin, the Sparticists acting as deep-cover intelligence-gatherers in the city break off contact. Troubled by this development, the Sparticists who remained outside the city to analyze data and help prepare for the invasion go into New Orleans to make sure that their packmates are all right. When they don't return either, the elders planning the invasion put their plans on hold until they can find out what happened. They call upon an even more specialized pack of infiltrators from out of town to go to the Sparticists' haven and try to discover and put right whatever has gone wrong.

The Glass House

A popular illusionist once designed a magic trick that causes a caged elephant to disappear in the blink of an eye. The high cage with its thick wooden bars has only two sides showing, with the walls angled toward the audience so that the cage's only corner faces outward. Essentially the cage is a wide "V" with the top facing the rear of the stage. Plants and fake jungle accouterments apparently cover the cage's interior and exterior to add atmosphere, but that is actually part of the magic trick. The magician waves his wand, and with a flash of blinding light and smoke, the elephant is gone.

Naturally, of course, the elephant is still there. The trick is that long-strip mirrors are hidden behind the cage's bars on swing hinges. When the pyrotechnics go off, momentarily blinding the audience, the mirrors swing out to cover the spaces between the bars. Suddenly the mirrors reflect the faux tropical setting outside the cage, giving the illusion that the interior still has its plants and scenery sans the elephant. Because the walls are angled away from the audience, they never see their own reflection.

That's the wonderful thing about mirrors. They show you the truth, or they show you what you want to see. Either way, the mirror never lies. You deceive yourself.

Resident

Jesse Van Reginald grew up in the tumultuous era near the 20th century's mid-point. While most people remember WWI and WWII, Jesse was too young to fight or suffer from the conflicts that raged on the other side of the Atlantic. Instead, he grew up admiring the skillful legerdemain of men like Dante, Blackstone, Dunninger and Houdini, and he taught himself the basics of magic. As he grew older, Jesse gravitated toward illusions, producing remarkable and imaginative feats of mirage on par with greats such as Kellar, Thurston and Copperfield. Unfortunately, any potential for prominence or fame died when Jesse did, impaled on the fangs of a frenzied Toreador who came to her senses just in time to do the "humane" thing when she found Jesse dead in her arms.

The Becoming was excruciating, for compared to the chimera and whimsy of the Ravnos or true magical acumen of the cloistered Tremere, Jesse found himself nothing more than an unimaginative hack. The Kindred were not impressed by parlor tricks (having seen true magic), and performing for mortals would have constituted a breach of the Masquerade. Certainly, his newly acquired bearing would allow him to "control the audience," as an axiom of magic demanded, but it was a wasted gift. Jesse found his creative spark crushed under the weight of his dead soul.

With some property and a decent inheritance from his parent's will, Jesse instead opened a small hobby and magic store to provide him a partial income. He sold devices for stage magic and offered night courses for people, eventually making enough to invest in a bar with a small stage. For the past few decades, the bar has been an intimate but popular venue for local comedians and magicians, while Jesse's adjoining magic store has grown into an affluent business catering to clients across North America (through mail orders and Internet shopping). Both businesses are lucrative enough that Jesse bought the buildings from their landlords, hired managers and employees to man them, and moved above the stores into the communal second story. He still earns a steady enough cash flow to exist as he pleases.

The buildings themselves are in an older section of New Jersey dating back to the early 20th century. The neighborhood is still popular, however, and it caters to trendy twenty-somethings who frequent the local bars and dance clubs. The store, The Magic Rabbit, is open until midnight given the volume of street traffic, while the bar, Faust's Pub, stays open for as long as local liquor laws allow. This neighborhood is part of accepted feeding grounds and the place of choice for young Kindred (Toreador and Ventrue mostly).

Appearance

From the outside, both businesses are situated in adjoining street houses dating back to the early 20th century. The exteriors still have a brownstone façade, bay windows jutting out and stairs to reach the elevated front entrance. The basement is half-exposed above street level. Maple and stained cherry wood still covers the interior, making it just dark enough to lend the store and bar a comfortable, intimate ambiance. Aside from that, neon signs decorate the large windows, barrel-vault awnings cover the stairs, and two decorative poles with glass-covered display cases advertise upcoming performers and store hours.

Jesse's haven is situated above the store and bar even though the two locations are in separate but adjoining buildings. Officially, management lists the second and top story of each as storage space, but Jesse hired private contractors to knock down the second story walls, creating one open floor between the two buildings. Neon beer logos or images of a magician's hat and cards also cover the second story windows, which are all painted black on the inside.

Because this neighborhood is part of the Rack, local Kindred of influence use their contacts to ensure that Faust's Pub and The Magic Rabbit remain free of close scrutiny. Of course, Jesse owes a few boons around town for such favors, and he is slowly repaying each.

Layout

The inside of Jesse's haven is more than a testament to his skill, it is his protection against an evil world that truly frightens him. In the course of his decades, he has witnessed and escaped many attacks, between persistent Sabbat incursions, assaults by vampire-hunters and the machinations of would-be Kindred usurpers. Never a fighter, Jesse learned to protect himself with the only tools and skills available to him, those of deceit and misdirection. Simply trying to make a haven impenetrable would have been either overly expensive or virtually impossible for him given the wide field of Kindred abilities that exist in the modern night. Instead, Jesse chose to cover his haven with wall-to-wall mirrored paneling.

Curved and flat mirrors drape Jesse's haven on every surface, including the floor, ceiling and walls. Every corner even has an angled mirror. The effect? Through these properly positioned mirrors, Jesse can see into every room of his home depending on which way he is facing. While this kaleidoscope of images would be maddening to the uninitiated, Jesse is intimately familiar with every reflection because every angle is deliberate. In fact, the haven's interior took years to construct and arrange because Jesse had to account for a multitude of factors.

Even more important than being able to see everything at once, Jesse knows where to stand to avoid casting a reflection throughout the house, and he knows someone else's position according to which mirror casts their reflection. Finally, his décor is as much a part of the magic act as it is functional. The furniture acts like a visual anchor, immediately centering Jesse's perceptions and indicating which direction a person is facing. To prevent someone from moving things around, however, Jesse has had to bolt everything into the floor, from chairs, sofas and tables to potted plastic plants.

The ceiling lights are recessed and covered with a metal mesh, which makes destroying the bulbs either time-consuming or prohibitively noisy. Each mesh has a small keyhole for a skeleton key that Jesse keeps in his possession. Additionally, while the mirrors may crack from a blow or gunshot, they will not shatter into pieces. Most are mounted and glued against boarding, so destroying a mirror takes about half a minute to accomplish because the attacker must tear the mirror down shard by shard.

False Rooms

Originally, the second floor of each house contained seven rooms of varying size, meaning that Jesse's entire haven comprises 14 rooms. Because Jesse was creating as many reflective surfaces as possible, he left many rooms completely empty and converted the larger rooms into smaller chambers and hallways through false walls. Additionally, he removed most doors (except when they served a purpose) to avoid someone altering the sight lines by simply closing a door. This adds to the haven's illusion of complexity and space.

The Hallways

The different hallways contain circular mirrors mounted around half-pillars, which in turn help bounce reflections back and into the different rooms. Jesse wanted to avoid long or central access ways through the haven, much like a house of mirrors or a glass maze has a multitude of turns and twists to disorient people. Therefore, the term hallway is accurate in that the areas are actually short passages between rooms. The contractors built walls to exact specifications (believing they were making a funhouse maze), either blocking hallways or creating new ones, while Jesse covered them in mirrors.

LIVING ROOMS

Jesse built two living rooms on opposite ends of the house, both with matching furniture, but set in mirror opposition to one another. This arrangement often confuses visitors and victims, distorting any anchor points they might have been able to establish. The only difference between the two is a hidden cabinet in the north living room. The cabinet's door is actually hidden along the seams that separate two mirror sections. The lock is a simple push-spring mechanism, allowing Jesse to open and close it without handles.

The cabinet's interior hides Jesse's toys, including a 10-year-old 26" RCA television set, a Samsung turntable and a large sampling of Big Band, Swing and Jazz-era vinyl records. He also owns two old speakers, a fairly new Hitachi VCR with a small collection of tapes on stage magic, and a satellite splice feed through the pub. Jesse lacks many luxuries in unlife, but he is fond of the ones he has, and he rarely replaces them until they are beyond repair.

Scattered throughout the same living room are six push-panel mirrors that hide Escher-like drawings, or pictures of his parents and now long-dead mortal friends. All of Jesse's photos are black and white, and none were taken within the last four decades because Jesse has few new acquaintances. Vampires do not like being photographed, and most are too predatory to truly call any beings friends without blood entering the equation. Jesse does not hate being Kindred, but he regrets this pitiful existence in which his immortality brings loneliness.

KITCHEN AND BATHROOM

Jesse still maintains one bathroom and kitchen, with mirrors covering every available surface (including the countertops and cabinet faces). He converted the other kitchen into multiple false rooms by removing all the fixtures, while the second bathroom contains a Westinghouse washer and dryer. He keeps the fridge and cupboard partly stocked with non-perishables, even though the canned items are a decade old and the carbonated drinks have long since gone flat. Jesse, however, cannot bear a kitchen without food or a toilet that does not work (which he flushes every morning before going to sleep). Jesse believes that there is something terribly wrong in not having the mortal necessities around. He does not drink, eat or use the toilet, but he cannot cope with the fact that he does not need them anymore. So he lies to himself and says that he's never sure when he'll have to entertain a mortal guest. He keeps his kitchen in working order as well, with cups and dishes in the cupboards, cheap silverware in the drawers and food that will never go bad.

HIDDEN DÉCOR

While Jesse's furniture is in plain sight, he keeps his cabinets and bookshelves hidden behind mirrors so that his haven appears austere and lacking in any personal items. The only visible décor is large pieces of furniture such as chairs, sofas, tables, the occasional potted plant and six-foot floor lamps with rope designs (all of which are bolted to the floor). These touches are partly decorative, but they also serve as Jesse's visual anchor points in the different reflections.

Jesse is very clean, and he carries around a soft handkerchief to wipe away any smudges on the mirrors. He spends an hour each evening cleaning various mirrors as part of his chores, and he puts away everything he has used or worn to keep the environment free of telltale clues. (Books might indicate a hidden bookshelf, or a discarded remote control might start an intruder looking for the concealed television.) Because he is dead and does not excrete oily residues, he rarely leaves behind fingerprints to indicate which mirrors he has touched.

JESSE'S HAVEN

Hidden behind a mirror at the back of the southern house is the one room Jesse uses for his sleeping accommodations. Unlike the other secret doors and cabinets, this one is not mounted on a push-spring mechanism. Instead, Jesse can open the door simply by slipping a plastic card through a seam between two mirrors and tripping the basic lock.

Jesse's bedroom is cramped and cluttered with personal effects from his mortal years. In "protecting his haven," he keeps all his personal effects here, yet the decades of living in paranoia are taking their psychological toll. Jesse grows weary of being vigilant in his own haven, and he slowly allows more personal touches to find their way into the maze, like the books and CDs in his hidden observation room. Still, memorabilia fills every corner. Against one wall rests the bed and nightstand. A cluttered dresser and writing desk flank the secret door, while a small closet occupies the last wall. Boxes fill the remaining space.

Behind the closet's wall of clothing is a hole near the floor. This hole leads to a crawlspace between the wall and a mirror that touches upon the outside wall and a gated window overlooking the back alley. Although the window is painted black from the inside, a small corner is untouched, allowing Jesse to look outside before escaping through the window.

SECURITY

On the ground floors of each business establishment are stairs at the rear of the building leading up to the conjoined haven. Jesse uses the rear emergency exit of The Magic Rabbit to leave and enter unnoticed, and only he possesses the keys to the stairwell doors in either building. Both lower doors are electronically locked and equipped with a small security camera connected to the haven's observation room.

Jesse is all about tricks, so he employs misdirection in both stairwells. The stairs reach a small landing with a large metal door on the left wall. Each door is impossible to open; the locks are rusted in place and the doors seemingly open inward, meaning the hinges are on the other side. In truth, however, the "other side" is actually a solid, load-bearing brick wall. Both doors are fastened to the walls, so kicking them in does not work. The only way to notice this is if someone tries to kick the door open using a level-five feat of Strength. A level-three feat of Perception indicates that the bricks adjacent to the doorframe are buckling because of the pressure on them, and that whatever is behind the door is rock solid. There is no echo or reverberation of empty air. On an Intelligence + Alertness roll (difficulty 6) the person can figure out that the door is just a decoy to frustrate the stupid.

The actual door is in the wall opposite the stairs. A successful Perception + Investigation roll (difficulty 8) means that the character making the investigation notices a tiny plastic flap hiding the keyhole, or the door seam in the wall. Once unlocked, the door pushes open, but it also sounds the alarm warning buzzer. The buzzer is part of a typical home security system, so the intruder need only succeed on an Intelligence + Security roll (difficulty 7) within 30 seconds to keep a loud alarm from going off. The warning buzzer and alarm are both hooked to Jesse's remote, alerting only him because he does not want the police scrutinizing his haven. If anyone working in the store or bar hears the alarm, they have strict instructions to call Jesse's cellular immediately. Both the remote and cellular are constantly set on vibrate. Additionally, Jesse is a light sleeper, meaning he can wake up even during daylight when necessary.

Observation Room

Jesse enclosed one room in the center of his haven with two-way mirrors along its four walls. Inside, he can see his haven at every angle without giving himself away, though truthfully, this room is also his sanctuary when he wants to relax and not stare at a thousand saddened faces looking back. The entrance is a push-spring lock on one mirror, meaning the door is flush with the mirrored walls and indistinguishable from them.

Jesse tries to keep the observation room uncluttered to avoid obstructing his sight lines to various mirrors. A recliner, arm table with a Sony radio and CD player, a half-stack bookshelf and a spiral rack for soft-jazz CDs, however, have found their way here, allowing Jesse an escape where he can read and be messy in his own home. The observation room also has its own mini-television set mounted in the ceiling, which monitors the downstairs security cameras, and a control panel for the lights and various house mechanisms.

A Constant Affair of Misdirection

Jesse continually searches for new tricks to complement his repertoire, and he uses a remote control unit to control some effects. Since being a magician means being part scientist, Jesse is constantly researching new uses for reflections and light waves. He tests these new theories and applications on mortal victims that he occasionally picks up from the local bars (but never his own). The following are his favorites:

• Mirrors and Obfuscate: Jesse has a fair understanding of Obfuscate, enough to work it in with his parlor tricks and to use its disadvantages in his favor. By "vanishing," Jesse becomes invisible mentally, but because most people aren't even in the room with him, they still see his reflections. Anyone moving through his room, however, will come under the influence of his Obfuscate, which means that they will not see him or his reflections when the reflections instantly disappear. Suddenly Jesse vanishes from every mirror because he is close enough to the person to "insist" he isn't there. At this point Jesse can either move, reappearing elsewhere, or ambush the target, who is taken off guard by all the reflections vanishing simultaneously.

Taking this effect a step further, Jesse also uses Mask of a Thousand Faces to generate one face, while his secondary reflections reveal his true form. Anyone in a room with him, however, will notice that all the reflections look like the Mask. This is extremely confusing when Jesse looks like the intruder and hides within direct sight of his adversary.

• Tripwire: If Jesse knows he is dealing with an Obfuscated opponent, yet his own Auspex isn't refined enough to detect said opponent, he activates the makeshift laser tripwires he purchased through the bar as dance floor pyrotechnics. Of course, the lasers do nothing but bounce around and fill the rooms with red lines since they aren't part of an elaborate security system. Nonetheless, anyone who crosses a laser line while using Unseen Presence or Cloak the Gathering disrupts the beam and reappears. It is as simple as that.

• Muting the Reflections: Double-layered plastic sheets pressed closely together so that they appear clear cover several key mirrors. With a flick of the bottom on his remote, Jesse can open the minute gap between the two plastic sheets, enough to admit a thin layer of air. The basic result is that light passing through the first plastic sheet hits the layer of air and half the light waves are deflected while the other half continues on to hit the second plastic sheet, bouncing right back where they came from. The colliding light waves then (wholly or partially) cancel each other out. While the distance between the two sheets dictates what actually happens, Jesse's trick creates a startling rainbow pattern of reflected light (much like the rainbows on microscope films, but more vibrant because of the specific placement of Jesse's house lights). The other mirrors suddenly reflect this image, muting most other reflections and filling the haven with rainbow patterns. Jesse uses this effect to impress (or entrance) other Toreador and to distract himself when he is tired of staring at his own reflections.

• **Glare:** Several recessed alcoves in the ceiling hide funnel-style mini-spotlights stolen from a local theatre company. When activated through Jesse's remote, the spots emit a bright beam that shoots off the mirrors and fills the haven with blinding white light. This effect distracts and impairs sight (increasing the difficulty to any sight-based actions by two). Jesse, however, carries around polarized sunglasses to offset this effect. His favorite trick is to turn off all the lights for a minute or two before hitting his opponents with an unexpected glare.

• **Last Resort:** Through a well-connected ally at a New York special-effects studio, Jesse has six mini-charges of directed explosives that he can activate independently by remote. These mini-explosives are situated behind key mirrors overseeing corridors and confined rooms like the kitchen and bathroom. These mirrors are also the easiest to break. Detonating the explosives doesn't cause tremendous damage, but it does send out a hail of glass shrapnel that slices through targets, delivering 10 dice of lethal damage. Jesse only uses this "trick" in the direst situations, though for added effect, he might point at the target through a reflection, making it appear as though he has the power to make mirrors explode.

Story Ideas

• Jesse disappears from the local Kindred scene, and his closest associates grow worried that something has happened to him. After a little checking, the coterie finds that he was last seen the previous night when he entered his haven. The coterie must break in, find their way around the place and perform an effective search. If they manage to find the observation room, they discover Jesse in it, staked, in torpor due to injury or rapidly decomposing after having met the Final Death. Whoever did this to him, the coterie reasons, knows Jesse's haven fairly well and might still be hiding somewhere inside.

• Fleeing their lost territory in New York city, a pack of Sabbat Cainites take up residence in Jesse's town. These Cainites (i.e., the players' characters) come across Jesse while he's on the hunt and track him back to his haven. The next night, they plan to storm the place near dawn, put Jesse to Final Death and make his spacious haven their base of operations for future engagements.

• While members of the coterie are visiting Jesse's haven on some item of business, the Kindred of the city are caught up in a surprise Sabbat assault. The visiting members of the coterie are trapped in the haven with Jesse, and they must fend off a pack of Sabbat Cainites who've made their way inside. The remaining members of the coterie must get in to help their comrades without falling victim to whatever traps might be waiting for their enemies.

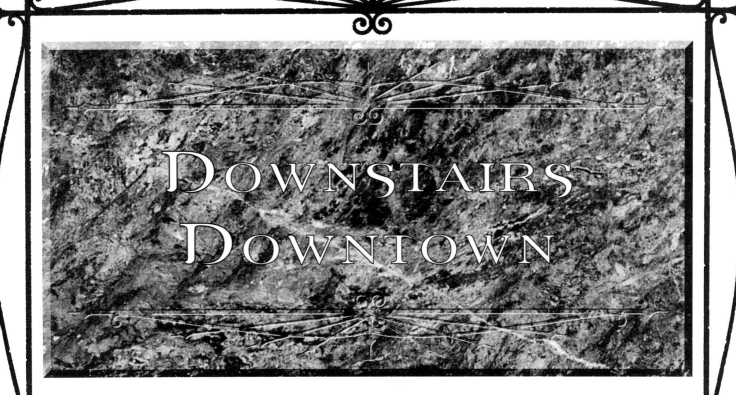

Downstairs Downtown

Anonymity can be a powerful defense. While many Kindred frequent trendy clubs and make their havens in upscale manors or modern homes, few would expect one of the undead to reside in a simple sub-street apartment. On one hand, nosy neighbors and demanding landlords can be a threat. On the other hand, a modest city can host thousands of similar sub-street apartment buildings, and this alone helps the resident blend in with the masses of the city.

In the past, sub-street apartments fell into the category of cheap basement rooms and trashy cellars rented out to poverty-stricken tenants. While this image persists in some parts of the world, the proliferation of high-rent condos and trendy in-city apartments — especially artists' lofts and homes for business executives who want to live near the central company office — means that a modest sub-street apartment can actually take on a certain panache. Old Kindred, still remembering the nights of basement apartments as cramped and dingy low-rent affairs, may occasionally overlook such possibilities. Young Kindred savvy to the changing real estate climate can score a reasonable haven in the midst of upscale urban redevelopment. In some city blocks, this haven can be just a short walk from a local Rack, which makes it a perfect place to lure away potential snacks. Kindred with an interest in businesses and banking find such a central location helpful as well, for the ease of making evening deals and meetings with various contacts.

Resident

Sebastian Wright, a communications engineer Embraced for a combination of intelligence and technical ability, uses a basement apartment in downtown Boston. The location affords him a place away from Tremere chantries and superiors, so that he can pursue personal interests. There's no worry about having some other Tremere poking in to fiddle with his electronics. Similarly, he doesn't need a high-profile residence, so he doesn't attract the sort of attention that a penthouse apartment or an aged manor might draw.

Conveniently located near the heart of the downtown commercial areas, the apartment also gives Sebastian easy access to local telecommunications concerns (where he can get in at night by posing as a consultant, thanks to his experience in the field). Doing so eases his acquisition of new electronics. Just a few blocks up the street, closer to the freeway entrances and exits, is a strip of bars and nightclubs under the shadows of the overpasses. This Rack provides ample hunting grounds.

Since he's not particularly old or tied down, Sebastian has no qualms about keeping his important possessions in one place. He doesn't fear any need to move quickly. His ability to influence people (with the Dominate Discipline) assures anonymity and helps to "convince" his landlord to accept money orders for rent.

Appearance

Located just off the Massachusetts Turnpike, Sebastian's basement apartment is one of several such hidey-holes often rented out to graduate students from the nearby universities. Just east past the river lies the famous Massachusetts Institute of Technology, a wonderful ground for feeding appetites both scholastic and hematological. North is the old university of Harvard, where a savvy Kindred can slip as an observer into late-evening classes on current economics and business. This central location also gives a good view of much of the city within just a few minutes' drive.

From the outside, the haven is a simple stairway leading underneath a large downtown building. Up above, a classy bistro serves coffee and aperitifs. Higher up still, small advertising firms fight for recognition among the many offices. At the bottom of the concrete stairs with their worn metal railing stands a heavy wooden door with no window, just a single eyehole and a metal bolt. The door doesn't even have a mail slot — the mail all goes into a mailbox in the lobby of the building.

Inside, the apartment walls are hard bedrock with a plaster covering and separating sheets of two-ply. Lighting comes solely from standard fixtures in the middle of ceiling fans, rather than from any open windows. The living room and bedrooms are carpeted in dark brown, and the kitchen and bathroom are both tiled. Tile makes for easy clean-up, and dark brown carpeting doesn't show bloodstains very well. The décor is pragmatic as well as tasteful.

Layout

A small basement apartment has several advantages that aren't immediately apparent. Since a Kindred has little need for a kitchen and really only needs a functional resting-place, any additional space is simply luxury. The primary bedroom holds Sebastian's bed and his few personal possessions. The second bedroom's been converted to an office for communications work, and the tools of that trade dominate the space. Furnishings are Spartan throughout, since Sebastian generally uses the haven only to sleep and conducts business at other locations. The only mandatory elements are protection from sun — amply provided by living in a basement with no windows — and enough décor to give the impression that someone "lives" inside, just in case an over-curious mortal should happen to enter.

Entry through the front door leads to a tiny hallway with the kitchen on the right, not even separated by a door. The hallway is unfurnished, and it heads straight into the living room. A door on the right side of the living room enters another hall that splits to the two bedrooms.

A worn-out, old couch with torn upholstery graces the living room. A faded blanket covers the couch to make it presentable, but Sebastian rarely uses it. The room has no dining table or chairs, and the small entertainment center across from the couch boasts only a lonely 17" television and a cable box. Sebastian built his own descrambler, since he found doing so easier than trying to get cable on a dead ID. Besides, if the police show up at his place, he has bigger problems than talking his way out of cable theft.

The kitchen requires only minimal touches. The cabinets hold a few boxes of non-perishable pasta and cans of soup. The refrigerator is stocked with only a bag of celery or potatoes — just to give the impression that someone actually uses the kitchen to prepare food. A clever observer will note that there are no measuring cups or mixing appliances to be found. Clean countertops are less of a give-away than dusty, unused ones, so the kitchen floor and counters stay regularly cleaned. The kitchen sink's disposal unit serves an important duty: It's the end for leftover bits of botched feedings or incriminating evidence thereof. A few cleaning supplies under the sink also help to remove the occasional bloodstain from the tile.

The bathroom, like the kitchen, has few amenities, and the bathtub is the only important fixture. Draining blood from bodies works well in a bathtub with a stopped drain and a lining of plastic garbage bags. Again, cleaning supplies are a necessity to keep the bathtub from becoming a filthy, grime-covered hazard of encrusted blood. While bringing corpses back to the haven is a *very* dangerous gambit, Sebastian likes to be prepared just in case.

The primary bedroom lies in the basement bedrock. Rather than just plaster walls, the basement's solid stone foundation lies between Sebastian's sleeping body and the outside world. This means that more than a flimsy partition keeps the sun out. Even with a sledgehammer and pick, it would take someone hours to dig down into the room. On top of that, the noise would wake even the sleepiest occupant.

The sole door to the bedroom has been replaced. Instead of the usual hollow wooden door, it's a solid, heavy wood slab with a bolt lock on it, just in case. Furnishings are simple. The closet holds Sebastian's gray business suits, as well as a few pairs of blue jeans and some flannel shirts for "dressing down" occasions. The bedroom doesn't even have any dressers. A single nightstand squats by the bed, graced by a lamp and whatever book Sebastian happens to be reading at the time. (It's even money whether he'll be into trashy science fiction or the latest communications engineering articles on any given night of the week.) The room doesn't have a phone, lest it interrupt Sebastian's daytime slumber.

Sebastian's only concession to thaumaturgic work rests in here as well. Opposite the closet lies an incongruous wooden locker that holds various ritual components, including a vial with bits of dried blood on the inside, a jar of pennies, a bottle of sawdust and a box of toothpicks.

Hanging from one wall is a faded, anonymous painting of a road leading through a covered bridge to a farmstead in autumn — a piece that occasionally reminds Sebastian of his human days, triggering lingering memories of his youth.

The secondary bedroom serves as Sebastian's personal research facility. While the Tremere keep their important occult materials in chantries, Sebastian still indulges in his hobby of tinkering with communications equipment. A large worktable holds neatly organized tools and current projects. These projects range from breadboards with soldered-together circuits to opened shell casings containing computer chipsets for cell phones and MP3 players. (Oddly, Sebastian can't stand to iron his own shirts, but he feels completely comfortable with a soldering iron.) A heavy tool case holds electric screwdrivers, pliers, clamps and an assortment of chips, transistors, resistors, capacitors and LEDs. Along one side of the worktable are a series of dowels, each with a spool of different-diameter wire. Resistance meters and waveform readers each have places comfortably secured on the back of the table, with connecting clamps in easy reach. In the cabinet on the left side of the room from the doorway are enough parts to put together a half-dozen amateur radio sets. The right corner of the room has a miniature refrigerator holding an assortment of batteries. Intruders will be disappointed that this Tremere doesn't keep much in the way of occult material in his haven. Instead, Sebastian uses chantry facilities when necessary.

A washer and dryer come built into a corner closet. Even though Kindred no longer sweat, clothes can still become grimy, and the businessman and dealer downtown needs to stay tidy. It's safer than going to an all-night Laundromat down a few blocks in the city, although anything requiring ironing or dry-cleaning is dropped off — irons are just a *little* too much for this vampire's aversion to heat.

Since the apartment is underground, it runs parallel to some of the city sewer pipes — the large ones that run under downtown streets. Obviously, there aren't any openings directly into the sewers inside this haven, but there's a manhole just a short distance down the street outside. If nothing else, Sebastian could rely on this risky escape route in case of an attack (provided he could get *out* of the close-quarter haven while it was under attack and make it to the manhole cover in the first place). It also means that the haven could be well within viewing range of any Nosferatu who might happen to shadow its occupant home.

Luxuries

Benefits of a basement apartment are few. Privacy is questionable, although it's almost certainly far from any other Kindred. The prime downtown location means it's a short trip to any important firms, shops, clubs and habitations where one might hunt or socialize. Sebastian eschews owning a car, instead walking or taking a cab. An upscale Kindred might prefer driving an expensive car, but that sort of attention-grabber doesn't fit well with the anonymity of the apartment and Sebastian's plans.

Fortunately, unlike crude accommodations, the apartment can carry a full suite of utilities, a phone and a computer line (with a high-speed connection, since nearby businesses in the downtown section and Sebastian's own technology-minded hobby demand that sort of technology). Recreational facilities, however, are minimal. Sebastian goes out for pleasure, instead of entertaining in.

Security

This urban apartment doesn't rely on sophisticated defenses or high-tech camera systems. It doesn't even provide the security of a gated community. Rather, it relies on being one of the last places that anyone would expect a vampire to reside.

A paranoid Kindred might install a set of locks or a camera at the door, but doing so would undoubtedly draw the attention of the neighbors and (if the Kindred hasn't already dealt with the owner) the lessor. Such potentially Masquerade-threatening attention doesn't merit the use of simple defenses that could easily be overcome by a Potence-backed attacker in any case. Sebastian's best option thus far has simply been to avoid being followed and to make sure not to bring anyone to the haven, aside from victims who won't be leaving in any condition to tell anyone about it.

Fire alarms come standard throughout the apartment. The price of having to put up with annoying beeping every few months while changing batteries is small next to having a warning of one of the few genuine dangers to a Kindred's haven. For truly important items, a small safe, embedded in the bedrock walls of the basement, offers a strong level of security. The safe is in the wall instead of on the floor so that it suffers less from potential flooding.

Because of the convenient location, Sebastian doesn't need special supernatural defenses. The sublevel building doesn't even need wards against sunlight — the bedrock stops that problem. About the worst an intruder can expect might be Sebastian threatening a (fake) blood curse against someone who comes inside unbidden.

Feeding

Obviously, a lone apartment doesn't present immediate feeding opportunities. It's best to stay away from the other tenants in the building, after all, as drawing down suspicion right on top of where one resides is never a good idea.

Fortunately, a downtown residence is in the middle of a high-density, high-population area. It's just a cab or bus ride away from neighborhoods riddled with the crime, homelessness and street life endemic to the World of Darkness. Any Kindred who can't find an addled, easy victim in such a place just isn't trying. (Such is especially true for those, like Sebastian, with even a little proficiency in the Dominate Discipline.)

When taste demands something better than an alcoholic binge, it's a short jaunt to some of the nightclub-cum-bars of the downtown Boston scene, where the university students congregate. The crowds gather there in the early evenings almost every night, so the Kindred can mingle easily. The "meet-market" atmosphere provides plenty of opportunities to pick up a quick date (and bite). It's even possible, though not recommended, to bring back a few friends for some late-night partying. Being in the middle of downtown, a wandering partygoer who's a few pints low can easily be packed off in a cab to somewhere else. And in the event of a little indiscretion, bodies do turn up in Dumpsters from time to time….

When he's feeling adventurous, Sebastian has even been known to hunt among local businesses in the early evenings, looking for some loner who's making overtime pay after hours. Unlike partygoers and derelicts, though, these people tend to be missed quickly, so hunting them is more of a rare diversion against the times when unlife gets a little too dull.

Difficulties

For starters, there's the ever-present problem of living in a complex surrounded by mortals. A few noisy neighbors can fray tempers to the edge of frenzy. Door-to-door solicitors may stop by during the day, though thankfully Sebastian can sleep through their knocking when he's inside the well-insulated inner bedroom (and dead to the world, with the sun up). Building inspectors and utility company workers are a rare potential interruption during the day for Kindred without connections to the right bureaucrats. Essentially, having a haven surrounded by mortals means having to interact with mortals. The heavy stone walls of the basement and the lack of windows offer a little leeway in case of frenzy, messy feeding or botched experiments, but extra care must always be taken not to arouse too much suspicion.

Basement-level apartments also have a nasty tendency to flood. For a vampire, this is mostly an inconvenience. Even if the place were wholly flooded, the Kindred would be in little actual danger. The potential loss of personal items strikes home most in this case, so personal effects remain stowed safely up in a closet or in high shelves of a cabinet. Worse, owners tend to become agitated when flooding occurs, and insurers might be called in to examine the place, carpenters hired to repair damage, carpet-layers brought in to replace destroyed flooring, and so on. Under most lease terms, this work will be done whenever the owner deems appropriate, which is generally during the day. Such visits can be disastrous, especially if a groggy vampire wakes up to the disorienting sound of floor fans or workers slogging through a few inches of water. In such cases, the best option may well be to cite the damage as excessive and to pick up and move on.

Many basement apartments hover on the boundary between classy apartment complex and low-rent neighborhood. The proximity of downtown slums greatly raises the odds of a break-in by a potentially hostile criminal. For a well-prepared Kindred such as Sebastian, this occurrence can simply yield a surprise snack. Coming home in the near-morning to deal with a drugged-out mugger or a surprised and armed intruder, however, can be more of a problem. Falling asleep in the face of opposition, or having to fight with the imminent threat of sunrise just outside, or even facing off against an armed human in a complex in which neighbors will probably hear gunfire, is just asking for problems with the Masquerade.

Maintenance

The first and foremost problem with keeping an apartment lies in the monthly rent. This entanglement can be mitigated to some degree by paying in advance with money orders, which don't require any special identification. Cash on the barrel is the Kindred's best friend, as lessors become remarkably less choosy when a tenant puts down good money up front.

If the Kindred doesn't have a false ID, establishing a lease can be tricky. Doing so may require the Kindred to dominate or force a blood bond upon the owner. Doing these things isn't necessarily a bad idea, but either can lead to later complications if the owner remembers too much, turns out to make a poor ghoul, or even if he simply sells the property to someone else.

The best bet (which Sebastian has employed on more than one occasion rather than resorting to more direct methods) is to establish a fake identity in the time-honored tradition. That is, he grabs a Social Security number from one of the young deceased, then applies for a new copy of a birth certificate, uses it to open a bank account and secures ID. (Of course, this identity can be traced to him, but these problems are common with anything that requires a semi-legitimate identity.) Kindred may or may not pass background checks. Again, having a few acquaintances in the right places can help. A persuasive, sociable Kindred may be able to get by on mortal references and natural charm, but this option isn't as doable for the old and the jaded.

Sebastian relies on his regular cash flow to make his cut. By working occasionally as a contractor on late-night projects — communications projects that he can do with the CAD software on his home computer — he can earn legitimate money. While money orders might seem a bit odd for rent, the landlord isn't too choosy with regard to an apartment that's usually rented to students or low-income families. As long as the rent shows up every month on time and he has the additional incentive of an occasional bit of Dominate to make sure no questions are asked, Sebastian has no problems keeping the landlord from looking too closely into his affairs.

Since Sebastian doesn't want to have a landlord or a maid service poking around during the day, repairs have to come out of pocket or through personal work. He has to take care of such mundane trivia as replacing light bulbs, repairing leaky faucets and otherwise dealing with the frustrating and potentially damaging problems that come with the property. Front-end work is, therefore, necessary to mitigate this. Sebastian was lucky this time around because he didn't wind up in a complex with too much bad wiring or piping. If he has to move in a hurry, though, such flaws could become a source of future frustration. It's difficult to detect some of these problems right off the bat — such as bad foundation work, mold in the walls or clogged sewer pipes — and Sebastian doesn't have the time or money to afford a home inspection before moving in.

Future

As continued telecommuting and the worldwide movement of labor sends companies to remote locations with cheap real estate, downtown developments may become run-down once more. The trendy, classy veneer of in-town housing could decline once again into slum-ridden squalor. As the surrounding neighborhoods lose their big businesses and acquire more McDonalds', pawn shops, antique stores and Radio Shacks, the property values will drop. Initially this drop would provide Sebastian with some advantages: lower costs and greater opportunities for feeding, since the increasing crime rates that come with the transition to a slum would cover up Kindred peccadilloes. In the long run, though, it's dangerous. Neighbors with good jobs and upward mobility aren't usually too nosy, but neighbors who are on the lookout for the next score or the next victim can become dangerous. While dealing with a few mortals here and there isn't too much trouble for the Kindred, even a slum landlord may hesitate to rent to someone who winds up having to throw down with the block's local gang.

Also, as property values deteriorate, maintenance becomes worse. Buildings change hands from responsible owners to low-rent slumlords whose only interest is to let rooms cheaply while providing little or nothing in the way of safety or maintenance. Poorly maintained building complexes can become firetraps. Indeed, the threat of fire may arise from an owner who hopes to capitalize on insurance before property devalues further. Lack of repairs makes flooding a more constant problem, and structural damage can even become an issue. Creaking beams and sagging ceilings do not inspire confidence in the dweller.

Worst of all is the specter of demolition. A poorly run building can wind up on the receiving end of a city "clean up" initiative — all too often, an insurance scam or corporate buy-out — and Sebastian may have only a few nights to find a new haven before the entire structure is demolished. Woe to the Kindred who sinks into a mild torpor of a few weeks' sleep, only to awaken as a wrecking ball opens the ceiling to sunlight.

Equally dangerous is the possibility of a takeover by a wealthier company that replaces the building tenants with higher-rent businesses. Such a changeover means renegotiating lease terms and putting up with inspectors who want to replace carpeting, shine up old fixtures and make all of the apartments more presentable. Added security means a new background check. Sebastian could even be turned out onto the street if the planners want to change the old basement rooms into something else — a gallery or trendy night spot, perhaps.

Story Ideas

• An elder Tremere needs to set up a modernized communications network at a new chantry in a neighboring city, and a coterie from that neighboring city must track down and convince this communications expert to do the job.

• The local Tremere hierarchy begins to suspect that Sebastian is bucking the system, because he's been spending too much time at his haven and they can't easily keep track of him. The coterie can gain a boon by bringing him back and "convincing" him to stay at the chantry, or by bugging his haven so that the Tremere can keep tabs on him more easily. But how do you bug a communications expert without him noticing?

• An unknown vampire is killing students at the nearby universities and homeless people within a several-block radius of Sebastian's haven. As the prime Kindred suspect, Sebastian is in danger of being put down by the prince's sheriff, so he must bring the coterie into the picture to help him track down, identify and neutralize the offender. They must then decide whether to help Sebastian clear his name (if, in fact, he's innocent of the crimes) or perfect the frame-up so as to take credit for ending the crisis by taking Sebastian out of the picture.

The House of Storms

Young people are so interesting. They're full of energy and vitality that older folks can no longer seem to muster. They approach life full of wonder and curiosity and limitless potential, even when they choose to hide it all under affected cynicism or emotionally safe apathy. Plus, there's just something about the fresh, blank slate of an eager young mind that's so attractive to members of older generations. By shaping and making a lasting impression on a young person, an elder can almost feel like she's shaping the future in her hands.

But beneath that lofty goal, vital youth emits a more basic type of attraction. It draws in the old, the hopeless and the seemingly used up. It reminds such a one that she herself was young once. That she used to be so energetic and alive. This is the true lure of youth. It's no wonder, then, that some Kindred are obsessed with it and consumed by it.

Resident

Kathryn Green was an unremarkable businesswoman who ironically made the bulk of her money as a result of the 1987 stock market crash. While everyone else was panicking and selling as if the end of the world was at hand, she leveraged all of the assets from the small firm she'd built in order to buy strategic stocks just before the government stepped in to bail out certain flagging industries. Once the storm finally settled, as she knew it would, 12 out of her 15 strategic stocks soared upward in value on the wave of government backing. In 15 days, she increased the worth of her firm by a staggering amount.

This accomplishment clinched the decision of her soon-to-be clanmates to Embrace her. They had been watching her for some time prior to the crash, and she had impressed them beyond their expectations with her foresight and unflappable calm in the face of potential catastrophe. Not long thereafter, in late spring of the year 2000, she was approached and made a member of the Keepers clan.

She adjusted well to the Becoming and discovered that she had a particular taste for fresh, hot blood with an identifiable tang of adrenaline in it. She experimented with different means of coming by such blood — purchasing synthetic adrenaline and adding it to blood heated in the microwave, or seducing biddable men in bars and feeding on them as she went through the motions of sex — but she found none of those methods entirely satisfying. Synthetic adrenaline did nothing for her, and the constant pantomime of picking up guys, letting them do their business inside her, then wiping their memories clean of the encounter after the fact became too cumbersome for the satisfaction it provided her. She wanted to find a way to make victims come to her willingly, yet still be overpowered by the excitement that would make their blood taste right.

Sadly, she had to admit that she was neither charming nor attractive enough to inspire such a reaction on her own, especially since she no longer had the allure of youth working for her. On top of that, an intuitive grasp of the Presence Discipline eluded her entirely. It took her the better part of a year, but she at last figured out a way to accommodate her feeding requirements, appear to be performing a civic duty while doing so and even make a decent profit at it. She chose a shopping center of flagging economic health, a place known as Broadway Corners not far from the thriving downtown area, and put her wealth to work.

At one time, the Broadway Corners shopping center was home to a second-rate grocery store, a Chinese dry cleaner and a dollar store only marginally distinguishable from a miniature indoor flea market. Before Kathryn came along, the place had been turning into a magnet for the city's growing Hispanic population, which was driving down property values in the surrounding neighborhoods and attracting other nickel-and-dime businesses into the area. This change in the community had begun to push out the reactionary white suburbanites, which was hurting the local economy because they took their money with them as they sought more homogenous pastures.

Since Kathryn renovated and redesigned the shopping center, Broadway Corners has become the home of a paintball pro-shop, a skateboard shop, a restaurant with a small bar, and the House of Storms. It is designed to attract the patronage and appeal to the sensibilities of the local white suburbanite (preferably ages 18-25) who wants to engage in socially acceptable counter-cultural interactions that aren't likely to land him or her in trouble with the local authorities. The products are mass-marketed, big-name items, the food is trendy, and everything costs a lot more than a dollar.

It took about six months for word to get out about the redesign of the shopping center and the entertainments it now offered. Since then, business has really taken off, due in part to the center's positive image in the community (which means, to the predominantly white community, that it seems no longer to encourage the growth of the Hispanic population). Another help to business is the number of schools in the neighborhood: two middle schools and one high school within a short driving distance, not to mention a college campus that's not too much farther away. Kids from these schools (who seem all too happy to spend their parents' money) are the primary target of Kathryn's enterprise. As it works out, the majority of the clientele, Monday through Friday, are under age 17. On the weekends, the majority of the customers are over 21. The parents of the kids who are regulars see the House of Storms as a pleasant alternative to their kids hanging out on the street.

To further community relations, Kathryn has arranged discounts on time and equipment rental at the House of Storms for the schools and local charity foundations that focus on troubled youth. Also, many of the local schools sponsor teams that participate in the House's tournaments. Prizes range from credit at the House and its pro shop, to gift certificates donated by other local businesses.

Kathryn has also backed the local anti-gang movement by starting an anti-gun and -drug program with the local police department. She has offered credit at the House and any of the stores in her shopping center, in exchange for any weapons or drugs turned in to the police, with no questions asked. Community and civic leaders have applauded this plan, even though the local community has never had much of a gun or drug problem. They see Kathryn's policies as an effective proactive solution that subverts any such potential problems before they arise.

Appearance and Layout

The Broadway Corners shopping center isn't especially remarkable to look at from the outside. It's small for a shopping center, and it stands off a major tributary of a main highway, rather than having a prime spot beside the highway itself. A mostly level sidewalk runs alongside the parking lot, and a couple of tall poles support the shopping center's marquee. The odd potholes and cracks in the parking lot have all been patched and re-paved, and the lines on the parking spaces have all been recently re-painted. Even the broad speed bumps in the lanes that divide the lot have been given a new coat of yellow paint.

The building itself is one solid unit divided into storefronts, demarcated by the differences in the size of the awnings that run along the front of the building. Colorful signs bearing the names of each business dominate the awnings, which are otherwise bland expanses of corrugated concrete. The storefronts beneath these awnings are mostly glass with stenciled advertisements or static window-stickers hawking the stores' latest products. The House of Storms is in the center of the strip, flanked by two smaller businesses that Kathryn also owns.

Road Rash

The former dollar store and a check-cashing office have been transformed into a combination music store and skate shop known as Road Rash. The place is currently run by a 21-year-old local named Billy, and it carries everything a skater and/or a music-lover could ever want. The selection of CDs ranges from suburban rebel classics — such as Kid Rock and Cyprus Hill — to harder, less parentally acceptable music — such as Kool Keith, Pantera or Public Enemy. Some of the T-shirts on sale here are from Graffiti, Porn Star or just about any other recognizable label that shouts attitude.

Road Rash also carries just about every type of boards, trucks, wheels and bearings a skater could want, from Zero to Alien Workshop. Anyone can find whatever she may need, be she a princess or a true skate rat.

With Kathryn's money and support, Billy has overseen the construction of several skate ramps behind the stores, in the parking lot that was once the sole domain of tractor-trailers making deliveries to the grocery store. Now, the miniature skate-park even has lights and its own outdoor sound system, and it sees use day and night. Because of Road Rash's popularity, it is almost always packed even after hours. All in all, Billy is well respected by the local youths, which makes him Kathryn's go-to guy when it comes to keeping new youngsters coming back to Broadway Corners.

One note of interest about Road Rash: a door in the back room, where inventory is stored, opens into a similar room in the rear of the paintball pro shop that is attached to the House of Storms. This heavy steel door was installed after Kathryn bought the property, and two deadbolts keep it locked when it's not in use. One deadbolt can be unlocked with a key from inside Road Rash, while the other can be unlocked with a different key from inside the pro shop.

Gino's

Gino's is a family-themed sit-down restaurant on the opposite side of the House of Storms from Road Rash. The dining room is divided into smoking and non-smoking sections by a wooden wall, on which pictures of legends from American history are prominently displayed. Large televisions hang in the corners of both sections of the restaurant broadcasting ESPN with subtitles scrolling across the bottom. A well-stocked bar takes up the very center of the floor inside, and circular and rectangular tables radiate outward from it. The place is normally busy and buzzing with conversations of its diners, and cute waiters and waitresses in yellow shirts and khaki pants constantly flit from one table to the next doing their best to be energetic and helpful.

Kathryn's haven doesn't extend physically into this restaurant, but she is a part owner of it, and she micromanages the management staff as much as she can get away with. The staff does pretty much whatever Kathryn wants, though, partly because being right next to the House of Storms increases Gino's revenue, and partly because she's usually right whenever she makes a suggestion anyway.

The House of Storms

The House of Storms is a former grocery store converted into an indoor paintball arena. To the customers, though, it's just the House. The first inner wall, which is visible through the glass facade outside, was painted white when Kathryn had it installed, but that has long since changed. Each team that wins a tournament gets to cover a section of this wall with its own brand of graffiti; the higher the stakes of the victory, the larger the space the team is given. So far, the most coveted spot to win is right above the entrance, which is currently held by a team known as the Wrecking Crew.

The Pro Shop

Once a customer is inside, a set of glass double-doors in this interior wall leads into the House of Storms. The first stop inside is the House's paintball pro shop. The pro shop has everything a beginner would need for his first game, and plenty of gear for even the most seasoned veteran (such as the newest Bob Long electric gun). The shop also carries a wide variety of pads, paint and rental guns — all of which come in new and used varieties. It also has the latest in air systems, and a customer can even special-order the color paintballs he wants.

On the south side of the pro shop is the repair desk, run by a man named Steven Alagore. Steve can repair just about any piece of broken or malfunctioning equipment, but if a customer only needs an upgrade or a modification, he can do that, too.

The Lookout

There are three other doors inside the pro shop. One, which is behind the counter, leads to the back inventory room of Road Rash. The second leads to the Lookout. The Lookout is an observation deck that used to hold the management offices of the grocery store and the grocery store employees' personal lockers, but which has since been converted for use by customers of the House. Up here, one can find vending machines, two pay phones, a few leather couches, and the latest and greatest video games. The most recent upgrades to the Lookout are two big 27" closed-circuit televisions. These screens allow spectators to follow the game that's going on down in the sections of the so called "War Zone" that are not visible from the Lookout, thanks to a pair of security cameras mounted in the ceiling.

The Manager's Office and Employees' Lounge

The third door out of the paintball pro shop opens to a hallway that leads past the employees' break room and into the War Zone proper. All eight of the employees at the House (except for Steve, of course) are good-looking young women who are fond of wearing tight shirts and "having a good time." Kathryn encourages the girls to be very friendly with the customers to keep them happy and eager to return. Considering the average age and temperament of the clientele and the popularity of the place, rumors abound concerning these girls' virtues and what they're willing to do for (that is, do *to*) the after-school soldiers who demonstrate the most prowess on the indoor field of battle.

Beyond the door marked "Employees Only" in this hallway was once the grocery store's cash room. Now it serves as the employees' lounge. The room has been carpeted, wallpapered and redecorated in leather couches and Ansel Adams prints. On the near wall sits a big-screen TV and all the electronic toys (a VCR, a DVD player, a

Playstation 2, a Game Cube and all the latest games) that the employees could carry from the local Best Buy. While this room is technically only an employee lounge, any customers who've spent an especially large amount of money at the House (or who have made *friends* with one of the employees) are allowed to play here as well.

On the far side of the room is the entrance to the manager's office, which doubles as the entrance to Kathryn's haven. The office is painted tan and white inside, illuminated by a single overhead fluorescent light. Its door is made of heavy wood set in a metal frame. Not being situated on an outside wall, the office has no windows. It's dominated by a large wooden desk and a row of filing cabinets holding documents that pertain to each of the businesses in the Broadway Corners shopping center.

On the back wall of the office, right behind the desk, is a heavy steel fire door painted the same color as the rest of the wall. The door and the hinges are oriented to swing the door outward from the office. By its placement, since the manager's office is located very near the back of the building, this door is meant to look like the old back door from the former grocery store's stock room. It's not, however, because that door is actually closer to the middle of the War Zone. The door in the back of the manager's office actually opens into Kathryn's private room.

Kathryn's Haven

The room beyond the door in the rear of the manager's office is split between an elegant bedroom and a second modern office, both of which are lit by Tiffany style lamps. The flooring is polished basalt, the furniture is of fine cherry wood, and the computer is a newly bought Dell Pentium 4. An entertainment center across the room from the computer contains a 45-inch HDTV with a Toshiba DVD-player.

A king-size bed, hand carved from English black walnut, dominates the bedroom side of the haven. The silk sheets match the cherry wood furniture. The rest of the suite is designed by the same artisan and of the same wood. A Persian rug decorates the center of the floor.

Kathryn spends most of her time in this room when she's working or relaxing. She comes out to deal with the managers of each of the businesses in the shopping center in their own offices, and she feeds in the employee lounge. She even makes the occasional nighttime visit to the homes of community leaders, pretending to have dinner with their families and reassuring them that the House of Storms and its satellite businesses are still having a marked positive impact on the local economy and providing a good influence on the youth of the community.

The War Zone

At the end of the hallway leading from the paintball pro shop and past the employees' lounge is the War Zone, which takes up most of the remaining space in the House of Storms. The wall that originally separated the grocery store's aisles from its stock room and inventory receiving area have been knocked down, giving the place the aspect of an empty warehouse when it's not in use. Music blasts over high-mounted speakers in the girders that support the ceiling, an eclectic mix of Ice Cube, Metallica, and Nine Inch Nails. Billy frequently brings over choice selections that have just arrived at Road Rash.

All of the walls in the War Zone are covered with plywood that has been bolted down. The walls and the high roof were then spray-painted with abstract urban color patterns of red, gray, blue and black just to add to the ambiance. Each wall has four "Play at Your Own Risk" signs hung up in plain view, each one of which is three feet by five feet. Naturally, every inch of the signs (as well as most of the walls and even a good bit of the ceiling) is covered in a multicolored stippling of paintball splats.

In the floor, holes three inches wide and six inches deep have been drilled into the concrete. These holes are laid out in an expansive grid that takes up most of the floor, and the employees use them to erect structures made from sturdy PVC pipes that have painted plywood panels bolted to them. These allow the staff to construct makeshift scenery, barricades, opposing fortresses and even a maze if they have enough time. These different structures then lend themselves to different firefight scenarios that the opposing paintball teams can act out rather than just running around squeezing off rounds at one another.

Feeding

Kathryn's unusual feeding predilection inspired the creation of the House of Storms, and she uses it for that purpose to good effect. She encourages her employees to inspire fierce competition in the paintball arena among the customers out there in lightning-fast, high-action battles accompanied by the loud, fast music blasting over the sound system. With subtle applications of Dominate, she has her beautiful, athletic female employees circulate throughout the arena cheering on especially intense exchanges of gunfire and inciting timid or overcautious participants to take action with breathy, good-natured encouragement. Doing so keeps the players' excitement high and their adrenaline pumping.

Then, once a week (or more often if business is especially good), Kathryn leaves a post-hypnotic suggestion in the minds of one or more of her employees to lure away one of the most active participants in the combat who's been temporarily sidelined by being hit with a paintball. As the player makes his way to the "tagged" circle to await his chance to get back into the action, the employee whispers a few words or even beckons suggestively to get the player to follow her into the employee lounge for a quick roll in the hay. Once there, she locks them both in and starts tantalizing him and leading him on.

This is Kathryn's cue to emerge from the manager's office, command her employee to sleep (which is the last part of her post-hypnotic suggestion) and feed from the excited, trapped player she's lured to her. Once she's finished, she changes the victim's memory so that he thinks he and the employee who led him away carried through with their rendezvous. She then does the same with her employee and returns to her haven through the manager's office. The manager, who is Kathryn's only blood-bound ghoul in the entire shopping center, then makes sure that the employee and customer get back to the War Zone without further incident.

Story Ideas

• To Kathryn's shock and horror one night, a young man she's trying to feed from fights her off and gets away from her. Displaying an unexpected reservoir of supernatural strength, the boy breaks free and pushes her away when she come for him a second time. She might have simply written the incident off as an overabundance of adrenaline except for the fact that the young man displays an equally powerful mental fortitude by resisting her subsequent Dominate commands as if she'd never spoken them. He then breaks open the door and flees into the night with his neck bleeding. Once she calms down and makes sure that no one else in the club seems aware of the problem, Kathryn calls the players' characters' coterie asking for help. Having pulled the kid's address from the credit card he paid with, she knows where he lives, but she's not about to go try to deal with him herself after her last botched attempt. The boy must be dealt with, though, in order to preserve the Masquerade. That's where the coterie comes in….

• A pack of Sabbat Cainites from a neighboring town hear about the House of Storms and come to Broadway Corners to get in on the fun themselves. Contacting Kathryn by phone (unaware that her haven is inside), they offer her a deal. If she'll agree to close down the House of Storms the following night and let them use it unmolested for a few Games of Instinct, they'll agree not to head to the House of Storms right that second and start playing their games while the place is full of customers.

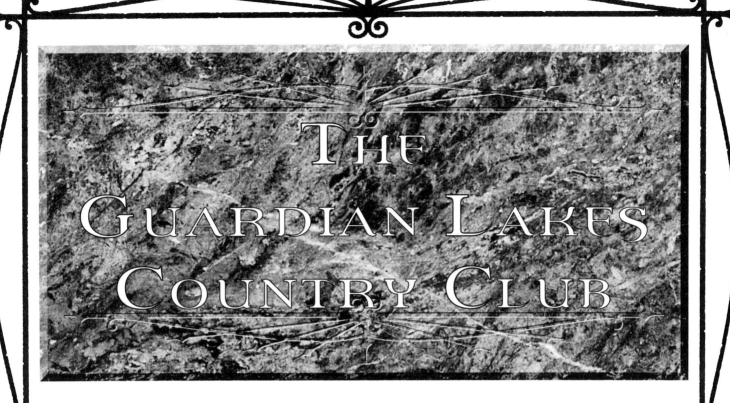

The Guardian Lakes Country Club

The Gangrel Kindred, driven by necessity into the cities but by choice attracted to the wilderness, often try to find compromises, and suburban neighborhoods, zoos or city parks are prime among them. For the innovative, the artificial gardens of humanity seem a possible alternative. Some Gangrel chafe at the "synthetic" creations, asserting that such places can't match nature. Other Gangrel, with some sense of irony, note that they're hardly natural creatures themselves, so they simply find solace where they may.

In suburban areas, the failing parks service can hardly keep up with the small territories that it holds. Funding is low, and government pressure to favor economics over conservation leads to continually shrinking preserves. Yet, just outside the big cities, wealthy landowners, recreation-seekers and sports aficionados maintain their own privately groomed landscapes. One such country club provides a domain and escape for a cautious Gangrel — as well as a haven and even a place of work.

Resident

Back before there was more than a small township in the area, Pahuska laid claim to the undeveloped lands on which the Guardian Lakes Country Club now sits. He'd roamed freely around the territories outside of what later became Charlotte, North Carolina. With the press of civilization, though, he increasingly found himself hemmed in and pushed away from the lands he considered part of his home. Realizing at length that the expansion of the city would pass him by — since, legally, he had little claim to the land beyond an old document of settler's rights — he hesitantly contacted an influential Ventrue with whom he'd had passably social contact in the past. Working in tandem, they used Pahuska's aged documents in conjunction with the Ventrue's money and connections to make Pahuska's ownership of the lands legitimate. The Ventrue set up the staffing and construction to turn the place into a park. In return, Pahuska was allowed to reside on the grounds and given a reasonable cover identity.

Now, Pahuska is just "Pat," the eccentric night groundskeeper/watchman. With his leathery, half-Native American visage and shockingly blond hair, he has an emaciated appearance that makes him look older than he really was at the time of his Embrace. Fortunately, he rarely has to deal with people directly.

Appearance

Immaculately groomed gardens, rolling golf greens, shaded hilltops and carefully crafted artificial lakes spread across 30 acres of fenced-in land. While it's not exactly natural, it's nevertheless a green and well-kept preserve, with strategically placed trees blocking the view from outside streets. Because the club lies just off a suburban one-lane byway, only a low fence surrounds it. Inside, the terrain favors low hills and lots of cut grass, bordered by heavy brush. Small lakes, streams and sand traps dot the course. Beyond the usual 18 holes are secluded spots out of the way from normal sports fare, perfect for walking, picnicking or dragging off an unconscious victim away from the public eye. In the evenings, the club grounds are considered a relaxing spot for the wealthy and jaded to mingle. The central clubhouse hosts small society functions, and it's not uncommon to see a few groups conversing out on the lawn, drinks in hand.

The club's central building is constructed entirely from expensive hardwoods with tasteful beveling. The windows are large and rectangular, while the doors are oversized and swing inward (the better to accommodate golf bags). Even the patio furnishings are decorated with carvings and designs. Carefully trimmed flowerbeds flank the entryways, and the maintenance trails are narrow and designed to remain unobtrusive.

The maintenance building resides out of sight from the club building, in a lonely corner of the grounds. In contrast to the rest of the place, it's a simple building designed as a shed with a room and a basement as afterthoughts. Aside from a "Maintenance Personnel Only" sign, it has no obvious markings.

While the club offers golf during the day, the occasional evening soirées attract the real influence. From society women looking to shine to old-time politicians rubbing elbows, the conversation and clientele becomes almost like a miniature roll of the rich and not-quite-famous. The club isn't necessarily open every night, but at least once a week, it's rented for some gala or ball — anything from a debutante party to a charity meeting of the Daughters of Columbus. Pahuska's Ventrue backer encourages this sort of thing, of course. Pahuska himself stays away from the club proper, instead looking for a rented limousine driver or other functionary who might not be missed *too* much if he were to cart one off briefly....

Layout

The fence has two gates: a main front gate with a security post to check in visitors and make sure that they're members, and an employee gate in back for workers and deliveries. The roads from both lead to a central club house and the pro shop.

The central building is an elaborate structure that truly shows off the wealth of the country club and its patrons. It boasts a lavish shaded patio, several rooms, a large downstairs foyer with a bar, extravagantly decorated upstairs chambers for private parties and balconies from which to look out across the course. All of these features are kept well-maintained, with trim, seasonal decorations — festive pastel ribbons near Easter, garlands and wreaths and a famously large tree at Christmas — and tasteful displays of trophies or sponsorship plaques adorning the walls. Each wall houses one piece of framed art as well. This art changes each month, each one being a donated display piece from a club member who's the current "hot thing" among local painters (and who makes sure that the work's price tag is prominently noted on the title card). A large fireplace dominates the back wall of the foyer, and it's there that members gather in the evenings with their expensive mixers to discuss their golf swings and to debate other business. Many different clients use the club building during the day and in the evenings, so it's stocked with a bar, a restaurant, restrooms, a manager's office, the aforementioned pro shop with an inventory room and storage rooms (for golf members who want to leave their equipment at the club).

Golf cart rentals are available at the club building, too. The golf carts ride across cement-paved walkways that cut through about two-thirds of the estate. Since the courses don't take up the entire grounds, some of the overgrown turf is outside the usual run of visitors, but nothing separates the wild, untrimmed areas from the green except for a lack of roads and mowing.

The tools of maintenance work and inventory for the pro shop and club all come out of the maintenance shed, which is out behind the club building proper and far enough away that a copse of trees keeps it out of sight of the visiting guests. This building also has access to the walkways, so that maintenance personnel can take carts to different parts of the course for work. The delivery road, by contrast, is a paved asphalt road that heads out to the back gate, so that delivery trucks can drive straight up to the shed. Pahuska keeps his few permanent possessions in a metal storage locker in the shed. They include ancient sets of bone beads, a chipped piece of turquoise that reminds him of his (now long dead) first love and copies of the paperwork that show the convoluted connection between his old paperwork and the current owners.

Luxuries

Privacy is at a premium here — evenings are rife with small parties, reunions and meetings of professionals who want to blow off steam or make deals. Late nights, after 10 PM, the club is typically closed, and then it seems eerily empty. The exceptions, the nights when a society party brings together the evening crowd, are very much well-lit, noisy affairs, yet the far-flung wooded areas of the grounds stay dark and quiet even then.

Fortunately, a groundskeeper has access to master keys, the better to do maintenance work across the entire building and all of the grounds. The club's computers have

Internet access, of course, and the staff offices have telephones, so there's no lack of technology. The club bar has televisions (for watching sports). Kitchen staff takes care of the dishes. About the only amenity missing is laundry, and the club actually has a professional service to clean staff uniforms.

Sadly, golf carts aren't exactly proper transportation outside the club grounds, so Pahuska must rely on other means of transit. He doesn't have the skill to wander about in animal form, but he rarely goes too far from the grounds these nights. If he leaves, he's likely to be gone for a week, staying wherever he can find a patch of ground. More affluent Kindred, such as the Ventrue and Toreador who occasionally arrive during one of the society parties, most often show up in their own expensive cars or in the company of wealthy high-society patrons.

Access to the groundskeeper's maintenance shed also means access to all the tools for upkeep of the green. This includes shovels, trimmers, waste receptacles… all sorts of devices handy for disposing of unsightly cadavers should lone witch-hunters show up while Pahuska is awake and prepared to meet them. All he really has to do is dig a hole in one of the far, tree-covered corners of the grounds, put a little caution tape around it, and cover.

Security

The defenses of a country club haven are twofold: its affluence and its prejudices.

While the country club doesn't have anything resembling armed mercenary guards, it does have regular security, contracted from a local company. The security guards are competent enough to detain normal people who might get out of hand, and they are professionals who remain inconspicuous so that club members don't have to think about their presence. Clad in bland suits with small security badges on their sport blazers, the guards remain unobtrusive, and they coordinate their actions through small handheld radios they wear on their belts. The checkpoint at the front gate always has a guard, even at night, and if any large-scale trouble starts, the guards know well enough to call the police.

Given the club's affluent clientele — which includes doctors, lawyers, judges and civil engineers, to name a few — a lot of influence passes through its gates. While the club's staff and manager don't have the ability to affect city policy, its frequent patrons make sure to use their influence on their own behalf. The club's existence spreads primarily by word of mouth. If you're an up-and-coming young lawyer, it's the place to go when the DA invites you for an afternoon round of golf. If you're a talented artist, you want to show off at the evening soirées to let the wealthy and powerful recognize you as one of their own. Should a disaster strike, it's well assured that the police and emergency services will arrive within a few minutes at most. After all, the people responsible for the cops' *jobs* play golf here. Anyone planning to cause trouble had best be prepared for a lightning-fast response. Otherwise, the police do their best to make sure that the interlopers are carried off quickly and discreetly, and there's little to motivate the police more than the possibility of a media nightmare featuring prominent citizens caught in a crossfire.

Because of the elite clientele, the country club doesn't let just anyone in to wander the grounds. Prospective visitors had best have a club membership, or else be visiting the place with a member. Such memberships don't come cheaply, of course, but the monetary cost is the least of matters. The club's board can pick and choose who's allowed onto the prestigious membership rolls. In this fashion, the established elite determine who's allowed to hobnob with the city's influential and who's to be snubbed. Anyone who shows up at the gate without a membership card (which may, depending upon the mood of the guards, be checked against the club's computer records), can expect to be turned around and firmly sent on his way. So, too, for those who prove obnoxious or difficult at the gate. Thugs and suspicious characters don't have a chance to make it onto the grounds. They'll be turned away, perhaps with the threat of police backup if their behavior becomes too raucous.

For the Gangrel resident, there's one other bit of security. Anyone looking for Kindred on the grounds will almost certainly head to the clubhouse first. The clubhouse isn't Pahuska's haven, though. Next stop is probably the maintenance shed. While it's possible to sleep in the basement of that building, which Pahuska does from time to time if he hasn't hunted successfully in a few nights, a competent Gangrel can use just about anywhere on the grounds as a bed by melding with the earth. Just locating Pahuska's resting place could take an entire day, and sniffing around the grounds like you're looking for buried treasure is a good way to have the guards ask you to leave.

Feeding

The first and most important feeding consideration with respect to this haven is, "Don't do it here." Bringing prey back to the haven generally isn't a very clever idea unless they're not leaving in any condition to tell anyone. With the high profiles and influence of the usual clientele, this haven's frequent guests *definitely* aren't safe to put on the dinner list.

Since the club doesn't include any sort of "company car," that means a lot of travel to reach places where feeding's a little easier. The suburban location of the club means that nearby neighborhoods tend to take missing people fairly seriously, and while there may be occasional classy restaurant blocks, there aren't seedy bars or clubs from which it's easy to lure off prey.

Of course, the evening parties might provide a small snack if an inebriated guest staggers out onto the lawn at night, but since scions of the upper crust don't usually mix with the service staff, even this sort of brief nip can raise suspicions. Still, if nobody's around, a dizzily drunken patron wandering the green may not notice or remember if a quick Kiss accompanies a little help in getting up and back to the club building.

On the flip side, Pahuska doesn't mind supplementing his usual feeding with squirrels, deer, rabbits and other wild mammals who make it into the overgrown areas. The use of a little Animalism can easily bring them to the fore. As it's the groundskeeper's job to make sure that animal corpses don't wind up on the green, Pahuska can simply toss the small corpses in the service Dumpster. Larger corpses can remain out in the deeper areas of the woods, off the beaten paths, where guests aren't likely to stumble across them.

Since it's best not to leave detritus where one eats, it's also prudent not to bring back bodies for disposal unless absolutely necessary. Only if Pahuska is sorely pressed for blood — such as after a nasty fight, or if some greedy rival should try to oust him from his haven — would he risk actually killing someone on the grounds. Similarly, he knows enough not to bring bodies back with him from outside. Access to the whole grounds combined with the tools at hand (wood chippers, chainsaws, mulchers and backhoes) make it easy to get rid of corpses, but a steady trickle of cadavers into the place would draw just a little too much attention. Each one brought in is a small chance that someone saw it, after all, or that some clue was left behind to tip off the authorities. It's better to leave remnants far from the haven unless there's absolutely no other way to dispose of the evidence.

Difficulties

Since so many people frequent the club, Pahuska must be very careful about the Masquerade. Traffic is low in the evening hours, of course, but he especially must still be careful of drawing unwanted attention. Most visitors won't give maintenance personnel a second look, but it's better not to press one's luck. Naturally, some landscapers work in the day. Pahuska nominally serves double duty as night security and as a roving troubleshooter for various problems that need fixing without disturbing the patrons. The guests don't appreciate noisy lawnmowers and maintenance drills while they're trying to concentrate on the course, for instance.

Transportation to and from the haven can be problematic, too, when Pahuska feels the need to travel. Pahuska must rely on more mundane sources like buses or personal vehicles. Even the nearest commercial complex is at least a mile away, which is too far to be caught away from the haven while afoot. Because Pahuska can sleep in the earth, this isn't as big a problem as it would be for some Kindred, but doing so is still draining. For this reason, Pahuska limits his trips abroad unless he's carrying enough money to check into a no-questions-asked motel.

Perhaps most insidiously, the clientele for this sort of club are also just the kind of people that other Kindred often try to influence. All of the assistant district attorneys, county coroners and business leaders draw the attention of Cainites who want to exert their wills on city developments. Any one of them could show up one day and be a ghoul, a newly dominated puppet, an entranced servant or just a subject of a little blackmail or bribery. Once involved in Kindred games, such mortals tend to become a little more aware of the presence of other Kindred and their influence. Worse still, such a tool could easily be a spy for another vampire, sent specifically to watch out for the Gangrel resident. While these moles might not spot Pahuska during the day, a little rifling through the paperwork of the club could turn up the oddities of its transfer of ownership, and a ghoul present for one of the nighttime parties might recognize the Gangrel by his somewhat *unusual* visage.

As the club isn't actually a "house" or other private residence, Pahuska also must keep the actual owners satisfied that he's not a trespasser or squatter. Working for the complex provides a convenient excuse for spending evenings there doing maintenance, but it's hard to justify sleeping on the premises during the day. Melding with the earth helps to mitigate this inconvenience somewhat, but even so, one must be careful to make a show of arriving in the evening and leaving in the morning, so as to pretend to head to some other domicile.

Fortunately, because of Pahuska's "arrangement" to remain a silent, hidden owner, there's no danger of eviction or losing the property to foreclosure, and the club itself handles all of the paperwork so that there's no hassle with trying to establish ID and legitimate ownership. On the other hand, that also means that the "real" owner (on paper) has the authority to be rid of unwanted guests.

Maintenance

The single most important task is keeping the continued goodwill of the manager. As a night-shift groundskeeper, Pahuska has a large amount of leeway. Nobody wants to spend all night overseeing the lawnmowing and fetching of golf balls. As long as the guests don't complain and the green stays neatly trimmed, there's no problem. That means staying out of the way of the paying members and doing a bit of grunt work in the evenings. Fortunately Gangrel tend to come from rough-and-ready stock not averse to a little labor.

There's no rent to pay or identification to forge. In fact, posing as a hired laborer can even have its advantages. Since expensive establishments will happily cut costs by exploiting labor, the Gangrel can eschew the need for any identification and just work "under the table." The paycheck may be smaller, but there isn't nearly as much of a paper trail. This has the disadvantage of lesser job security, but a manager who owes favors to the Ventrue who sponsors the place isn't likely to push the issue.

Keeping the grounds pretty much means making sure that the green remains presentable and playable for the membership. This gives Pahuska plenty of room to keep sections growing wild, as he sees fit, or to indulge in a little personal decoration of the club building as long as the management doesn't object to the design.

Future

The affluent clientele of an upscale country club provides well for future security. Unless they start taking their golf games elsewhere, influential members can make sure that the club is never bought out or re-zoned. It won't be bulldozed and paved over, and even if the management changes, there's little chance of sweeping alterations.

Successful clubs sometimes expand their grounds, which would give Pahuska additional room and the chance to indulge in setting the style for new areas. Nostalgic statuary or decoration may grace the sides of the walkways, or a few more lakes might be the order of the evening. As night groundskeeper, the Gangrel has strong input in future landscaping, since he'll ultimately be responsible for taking care of it.

About the only real worry lies in changing management or staff positions. A new manager may fire personnel, which can be awkward — or, more difficult still, try to promote a night groundskeeper to head groundskeeper, which means daytime work. It's difficult to explain away a promotion out of a desire to keep working nights. In either case, Pahuska would need to act quickly to cow the management or get out.

Story Ideas

• Pahuska finally starts gaining animalistic features that are too odd to conceal. He must fake his own demise and turn over actual ownership to another Kindred, who must then cover up Pahuska's continued residence there. One of the members of the coterie is in the running to gain ownership, and he must decide whether to honor Pahuska's ancient claim to the land or dispose of him outright.

• The Ventrue sponsor who helped Pahuska become a secret owner in the club decides to call in the favor by making the site Elysium and hosting an important Kindred gathering there. Pahuska enlists the coterie to handle security and make sure nobody gets out of hand or tries to molest his mortal guests during the evening soirée.

• A mortal gang shows up on an off night and vandalizes the place. Enraged at this violation of his territory, Pahuska kills one (or several) of them in a frenzy. Now the coterie must use its influence and Disciplines to help cover up the resulting mess, especially since the surviving gang members were witnesses. If all of them turn up dead under equally mysterious circumstances, the wrong kind of suspicions might arise. The coterie, therefore, must find a plausible way to cover Pahuska's involvement, in return for favors from him.

The Elevator and the Arrow

One of the fundamental aspects of a haven is the safety and stability that it provides for a Cainite in these, the turbulent Final Nights. Knowing, by virtue of what they have become, just how truly dangerous their world is, and faced with a worldview that has changed radically from the ignorant one they enjoyed during their breathing days, many vampires crave some island of sanity and isolation against it. Some Kindred, however, simply cannot stay locked away forever. They might be on the run, or they might simply be unable to resist the urge to explore and travel, but being cooped up simply isn't for them. Yet even those Kindred have no less a desire for safety and security than their more staid fellows.

And then, of course, some Kindred want it both ways.

Resident

Conrad Constantinos is a typical Ravnos in a number of different ways. He is a loner and a nomad, making his way from city to city with little reason other than his wanderlust and his abiding hunger. Conrad is, furthermore, quite capable of taking care of himself physically, a consequence of almost one hundred years of unlife and the need to constantly be prepared just in case someone finds out what he is or a hunt goes bad somehow. His hair is shaggy, his clothes are plain and hardy, and his eyes are sharp.

In his younger years, he loved his freedom to move through the night with little care other than the clothes and equipment he carried. Conrad eventually came to realize, however, that his independence provided potential enemies (such as Lupines and older Cainite predators) with an exploitable weakness. If they found out where he'd decided to sleep that morning, all they had to do was surround him and pick him off at their leisure.

Even though he was loath to change his wandering ways, Conrad realized he needed to change something about his unlifestyle in order to ensure his safety. He also wanted a place to call his own, a place that would ensure his privacy as the open road never could. Finally, even though he spent much of his time between hunts in rural areas, to hunt effectively and anonymously meant regular journeys deep into the urban sprawl — a place where he couldn't guarantee finding the soil necessary for earthmelding. He needed an alternative.

Not being one to rely on others' protection, Conrad searched for a secure haven that would also allow him easy egress should he need to escape in a hurry. He chose the abandoned overseer's office of a grain elevator in Iowa that had not seen use in over 20 years.

The Elevator

Conrad's skill with tools during life (he was a machinist) came back to serve him once again as he slowly and methodically modified the office over a series of weeks to serve his interests. Besides needing to shield the broken windows and cracks in the walls from the sun, Conrad also installed some simple and effective security measures for his own peace of mind.

Layout

Conrad's haven is built into the overseer space on top of the unused grain elevator. From this high vantage (almost 30 feet in the air), the managers who worked here when the elevator was in use could regulate and monitor the transfer of grain from the elevator into waiting train hoppers. Yet even when used most regularly, the offices were kept fairly Spartan. For Conrad's purposes, the room's most useful aspects are the many windows that provide at least a 270-degree field of vision. In his quest for a secure haven, Conrad was determined to keep the form and function of the room largely intact, concerned that drastic changes would ruin a tried-and-true design. Therefore, the Kindred did little to change the overall structure and instead focused on making smaller modifications.

Conrad's haven encompasses just about 400 square feet. Before his modifications, the chamber occupied about the same space as an in-city efficiency apartment. The haven itself is a single room, although the surrounding grain elevator and the still-functional railroad track that runs beside it create an image of a much more extensive haven. Conrad began his modifications by focusing on the large structure of the elevator itself, since it provides the only access into his haven (unless somebody wants to fly in, of course).

Enclosed stairs embedded in the grain elevator itself are the standard means of entrance and exit. Another smaller room at the base of the stairs provides a certain measure of security, allowing only someone with a key into the room and up the stairs, where another key opens the door into the haven. Each heavy wooden door has a built-in key lock as well as an external combination lock that Conrad added. There are no windows in the door or at ground level. Although Conrad used the heaviest metal and equipment he could lay his hands on in order to shore up the doors from the inside, most of his supplies came from scavenging, and he was forced to make do with inferior materials, such as aluminum. One advantage the scavenged supplies provide in lieu of physical protection, however, is that they maintain the illusion that the elevator and haven are in a state of disrepair, helping keep the idle curious from noticing the changes that Conrad has made within.

Once a visitor passes the ground level and climbs up the stairs (which Conrad has checked and rechecked for stability, lest they break one evening while he's climbing them), another door provides entrance into the haven proper. The door at the top of the stairs is similar to the one at the bottom, although another two padlocks secure it. For both doors, Conrad has made sure that the metal and the bolts that secure each of the locks to their respective walls are quite sturdy. A creature with supernatural strength would have little problem busting through the door or surrounding wall, but normal humans (and Kindred with only normal strength, for that matter) will be hard pressed to break them down or shatter the locks without some kind of mechanical device.

Conrad keeps the keys to both doors on a sizable key ring, which he keeps attached to a thick chain leading from a belt loop to his pocket. All the keys from both the grain elevator haven and the vehicle he keeps outside are on the key ring in random order. Even though Conrad can recognize each key at a glance, anyone not immediately familiar with the key ring will have to spend considerable time trying and retrying keys to break in on him (assuming they somehow managed to acquire the key ring). Of course, picking the locks is always an option as well. Picking the many locks on the first floor requires a Dexterity + Security roll against a difficulty of 6, and picking those at the top of the stairs (the locks that lead directly to the haven) requires a success at difficulty 7. The locks to the recreational vehicle are mostly factory-installed, so they present only difficulty 6.

Inside the grain elevator haven, Conrad keeps little in the way of furniture. He keeps most of what he values on his person at all times, including his bedding. One of the few luxuries that Conrad truly relishes is the ability to occasionally sleep on an actual mattress. Scrounging at a not-too-distant city dump and spending some of the little money he has, he's brought an old box-spring and mattress up into his haven, and he uses them without a frame. This one luxury dominates the corner nearest the door and has a sizable indentation in the springs from repeated use.

The corner of the office opposite his bed is devoid of anything so that Conrad can uncensored throw his traveling equipment out of the way once he enters the room. Conrad likes the ability to enter and immediately discard the trappings of his travels, and his behavior borders on the obsessive in order to keep that particular corner of a given haven free from clutter. Even the few times he allows another Kindred into his haven, he thinks nothing of yelling and overreacting to keep his guest away from the corner. This habit also helps ensure that his most prized possessions are only rarely away from his immediate vicinity and less likely to be stolen.

Next to the mattresses, diagonally opposite from his empty corner, Conrad keeps a makeshift desk. Made out of wooden pallets, cinder blocks and large cable spools, this desk is quite simple and workmanlike, if a bit oversized. He uses the desk to keep a few journals he occasionally writes in when he's got nothing better to do. In the pages of his journals, one might find his cliché observations on unlife, spiteful and cruel stories about some of his victims (which Conrad seems to find funny), and his occasional experiences meeting other Kindred. Also wedged in the journals are random pieces of paper where Conrad has written important notes to himself on where to find good hunting grounds and who might already claim them as domain. Nowhere in his notes, though, are warnings to himself to stay away from said grounds. Instead, he's listed tips and warning signs on how to avoid other Kindred when he's hunting in their territory.

Beyond the desk littered around the haven are old paperback books whose cover prices range from 50 cents to four dollars. Conrad seems to prefer literature that focuses on travel, as many of his books are copies of Jack Kerouac and John Steinbeck novels in various states of ruin from overuse. One can also find amid the pile several yellowed newspapers dating back at random intervals to 1969, as well as most of the pieces from four different jigsaw puzzles. Sometimes, one might even find a half-finished jigsaw puzzle spread out on the desk between clumps of mismatched pieces. Conrad also keeps a number of decks of cards with which he plays solitaire over and over and over.

The final major feature on the inside of his grain elevator haven is a large metal and plastic cage that could easily fit specimens of the largest breeds of dogs. Conrad acquired this cage by happenstance one evening from the side of the road at the site of a minivan accident. It is still quite beaten up from being thrown clear of the back of the vehicle it was in, and the tears in the wire mesh that Conrad had to twist back together and bind securely are obvious to the untrained eye. The cage smells of all sorts of refuse, from animal droppings to human sweat and blood. When he's staying at this haven, Conrad normally hunts within the confines of a nearby city, but not exclusively. His modus operandi has also been known to include stalking and capturing at least one good-sized animal to hold it over in the cage in order to provide a backup resource of vitae. Although animal blood (which is what he usually ends up with) is not as satisfying as the rich vitae of a human, it serves its purpose if he doesn't feel like going out that night.

Conrad binds any captured creature inside the cage with a length of thick insulated wire to a ring in the floor that comes up through a hole in the cage bottom. Conrad tries to avoid taking family pets or working animals as his backup, but he refuses to hunt for more than two nights for something that's just supposed to function as a convenience. He will grab just about anything by the end of that second night.

Additionally, Conrad is not above kidnapping a homeless person or wayward drunk should the opportunity present itself (though he usually needs the recreational vehicle to transport his human victims without anyone noticing). Regardless of what he captures, he does not intend to allow it to leave once he brings it to one of his havens. Conrad has no wish to compromise his security by having an escaped dog lead someone straight back to him, and he is especially loath to allow a human to live after seeing the inside of his haven and discovering what he is. Therefore, even if he is too full to bleed them dry, he snaps the neck of whatever helpless creature he has captured when he leaves, and disposes of the body in the nearby dump or other out-of-the-way place. If he's in a real hurry, he'll just drop the body in a drainage ditch by the side of the road far from his haven, then head out in the other direction.

One of the major modifications Conrad has made to his grain elevator haven is a secret exit. His haven is not all that far away from the nearby railroad track (which is still in use, but which obviously doesn't stop at the elevator any more); the modified exit is many feet above that track. In the wall facing the track, Conrad has built a concealed door three feet square. The door is made to look as much like a part of the wall as possible, which was a relatively easy task due to the conglomerate nature of his haven.

One risk Conrad takes with this exit is that the door is never locked, because a lock might give away the door's presence. Instead, Conrad relies on placing his large ramshackle desk in front of the door to help disguise the exit. Since the door opens inward, he's also rigged up a metal bar to brace it against forced intrusion from outside. He uses the small door as a last-ditch escape route from which he can fall to the ground and then rely on the Discipline of Fortitude to help avert any major injuries. If his timing is right, he can also use the door for easy access to a train as it makes its way past the haven. Conrad has taken to occasionally hitching rides on trains to get quickly from one part of the city to another, jumping off and landing in a rolling heap of flailing arms and legs just as the train speeds by his destination. He is especially likely to use the local trains when he has parked his recreational vehicle far from his haven in order to keep anyone from realizing that it is his.

The 1981 Pace Arrow

Despite the relative isolation and security of the grain elevator office, staying continually at that isolated haven started to wear Conrad's nerves thin. A wanderer at heart, staying in one place for more than a few weeks just irked him. Conrad decided that always hunting in the same city was simply not a great idea, and he began looking for a way to build a mobile haven. In the end, he scraped together a few thousand dollars over several years of moderately successful grifting and outright robbery of his victims, and he bought a dilapidated recreational vehicle that he could modify to his own ends.

Appearance

When Conrad's wanderlust strikes and he can't stand to be cooped up in the elevator office, he uses his RV, a rusty, grimy 1981 Pace Arrow, to move about the country. The RV is slowly falling apart because Conrad bought the vehicle almost 10 years ago when it was already beginning to show its age. The Pace Arrow is dirty, and it belches puffs of dark exhaust whenever Conrad accelerates, but he's a good enough mechanic to keep it operational nonetheless. The windows are deeply tinted and curtained inside, both of which details hide the fact that plywood covers the inside of the glass in order to prevent any light from getting inside while he's sleeping. The driving cabin and rear of the RV are completely separated by a makeshift door that Conrad can secure from inside every day.

Layout

Inside the RV is a large bed that sags in the middle from repeated sleeping. The frame is built into the floor and wall of the vehicle, but the mattress was missing when Conrad bought the thing. He had to make another trip to a junkyard and scrounge up the lumpy, blue-pinstriped pad he's got now. Conrad keeps a sheet over this bed made of sewn-together pieces of clothes that he has collected from various victims in other Kindred's domains. Conrad particularly prizes the patchwork sheet as a trophy of his many conquests, and he refers to it time and again in his journal back at the elevator office.

Beside the bed, an old La-Z-Boy chair dominates much of the interior nearest the driving cabin. The tan plush seat is losing stuffing in a couple of noticeable areas, and a faded red stain covers the right arm and some of the back. When he's traveling particularly long distances, Conrad occasionally restrains a captured victim in this chair for a night or two; the stuffing is coming loose in the areas where such victims struggle against the ropes that hold them down. The interior of the Pace Arrow smells, as well, because of Conrad's neglect and unwillingness to do more than tidy when he feels like cleaning. Electric camping lanterns light the RV at night when Conrad is staying in, and the illumination leaves numerous long shadows across the messy interior. Posters of movies he's seen on the road, maps and pilfered AAA guidebooks, and Polaroid pictures of the places he's been all crowd the wall space, creating a chaotic atmosphere. The tape holding up many of these decorations is ancient and yellow from years of temperature fluctuations and moisture, so any sudden stop or start (or even traveling over a particularly bumpy road) is likely to send them cascading to the floor.

Conrad moves from region to region in the RV, scouting the place out to hunt as soon as he enters a new city, but usually not staying longer than a few weeks. While he doesn't stray out into the deep wilderness (which he feels would be tantamount to ringing the Lupines' dinner bell), he travels mostly via interstate and parks in nearby popular campgrounds or travelers' rest areas. When he can, he parks near copses of trees or under an overhang to provide another layer of passive defense against the deadly sun.

This is not the first vehicle that Conrad has used, but it is his first RV, and it's the first vehicle he's ever owned. He traveled before by stolen car or van (when he could get his hands on one), wrapping himself in heavy blankets and curling up in the floorboards or trunk to sleep. Those methods proved too risky, though, since he kept having to change vehicles in order to keep from getting pulled over for driving cars that had been reported stolen. Plus, even in his wandering and rambling, he craved something stable that he could call his own. Recognizing its potential to be just what he'd always wanted, Conrad fell in love with the Pace Arrow the instant he saw it. He may not be able to keep it forever (given the vehicle's failing condition as well as the fact that it might eventually connect him to some murder he's committed on the hunt), but he'll keep it as long as he can. Once it's past its prime, he'll go looking for some naïve mark whom he can convince to buy the thing off him in order to refurbish it as a vintage automobile. If he can work that out, he'll start all over again with a new(er) RV just like he did with this one.

Security

The greatest danger to both of Conrad's havens is the sun. By and large, most people easily ignore the nondescript grain elevator and Pace Arrow, so he's not in much danger of being discovered. The shoddy, run-down look of both of Conrad's current havens, however, means that any number of cracks and crevices might allow deadly shafts of sunlight inside while Conrad is sleeping. Even the advantage of having a good view of the landscape is canceled out many times over by the fact that windows are killers in a Cainite's haven. To this end, Conrad has spent countless hours over countless nights while refurbishing the havens to make sure that they are sun-proof.

The first line of protection against the sun is Conrad's liberal use of industrial caulk and corrugated aluminum to patch the many holes in the walls of the elevator and the interior of the recreational vehicle. Conrad's excessive use of caulk has left the metal walls in his grain elevator haven a patchy off-white mess rather than their former industrial gray. At each and every joint where a wall meets another wall or the ceiling, Conrad has traced and retraced the spot with caulk. Furthermore, any holes in the surface that are thicker than a pencil lead have been patched with metal sheets of various sizes, all larger than necessary. Conrad has given the inside of his Pace Arrow the same going-over, which lends a certain similarity to the interiors of both of his havens.

In both havens, Conrad also keeps a number of rolls of duct tape to immediately (albeit temporarily) patch any cracks that may form without his attention. After he gets home to the grain elevator and flings his knapsack into its special corner, he methodically goes over the walls and ceiling looking for new cracks or old ones that have expanded past his patches. He takes care of any new cracks he discovers with duct tape, then immediately sets out to see if he can get his hands on some caulk or bits of scrap metal. He is a little less diligent when he inspects the recreational vehicle, but he does engage in a weekly maintenance routine in which he looks up and down the interior and living space for cracks. Naturally, he patches any he finds.

Also, Conrad has spent a good deal of time fixing up the windows in both of his havens. In the grain elevator haven, each window has a corresponding piece of plywood that Conrad cut and shaped with a handsaw so that he can fit them nearly seamlessly in the panes each morning.

Each piece of plywood is set on a pair of hinges at the top, which keep the board securely in place and make it easy to lift out of the way and secure to a hook in the ceiling. After swinging the plywood down and shoving it into place, he then duct tapes the edges just to make sure that there is no open space between the board and the pane. Every evening when he wakes, he simply takes down the tape and lifts the boards from those windows that he wants to see through. Only rarely does he actually open more than two windows, though, reasoning that constantly adjusting and readjusting them is simply an invitation for a mistake to occur.

In both of his havens, his last lines of protection against the sun are three large fire blankets that he acquired from the widow of a city fireman. Conrad sleeps with each of these blankets piled on the other, ensuring that even if he does happen to miss a crack in the walls or the windows, his body is well protected while it is under the closely knitted fabric. With no need to breathe, he can easily keep all of himself under the blankets for the entire day. The only downside to this measure is that if he should wake because someone has broken into his haven aiming to do him harm, disentangling himself from the blankets in order to defend himself could prove somewhat troublesome.

Feeding

For the most part, Conrad attempts to hunt near his havens (such as where his RV is parked), but not so near that he risks attracting attention back to them. Not only does he rely on the security of being able to quickly escape to the controlled environment of the sprawl should something go wrong, he just doesn't want to put up with the hassle of having to kill every fool who comes nosing around his haven when he wants to be alone. After all, there's only so much that one Kindred can eat.

Conrad relies on the slowly expanding suburbs within a few miles of the grain elevator for feeding when he's staying at home. His utilitarian attire and the trappings of the road he carries convey the image of a poor drifter or a local bum — that is, someone to be ignored. Conrad does little to dissuade his victims from this impression, and he uses it to great effect in order to gain the confidence of others in the area who are themselves poor. He uses these folks as contacts on the local scene to keep him apprised of any changes that might have taken place while he was away traveling.

When Conrad is low on money, he becomes a more social predator. He selects a likely mark (usually a lonely older person who's not afraid of strangers) and does what he can to bring that person into his confidence briefly. He then plays the role of a war veteran down on his luck looking for money or a hot meal somewhere. Then, using his charm and predatory guile, he pretends to connect with his mark emotionally and tries to find a way to get him or her alone. The inevitable then happens, and Conrad leaves his mark, often dead or near death, in her own bedroom and certainly poorer.

Story Ideas

• The scourge of the chronicle's city setting reports to the city's prince that a Kindred outsider has been raiding his domain and kidnapping people. Evidence suggests that the interloper is still at work in the city and operating out of a certain range of neighborhoods, but it isn't clear who he actually is. Therefore, the prince and the scourge authorize a coterie of willing Kindred to stake out those neighborhoods and find out who's been violating the Second Tradition.

• Needing desperately to flee the West Coast through the rural Midwest but terrified of being savaged by Lupines for their trouble, a small pack of anarchs happens to hook up with Conrad, who's at the end of an extended trip. Considering him an accomplished traveler who knows not only the best feeding spots in the desolation along the highways between major cities, but also how to safely avoid the rampaging Lupines that the woods are undoubtedly crawling with, they agree to meet his high cash price for taking them anywhere. The trip is hardly peaceful, however. The places Conrad takes them to feed are technically other vampires' domains, and the Lupines are quite a bit more aggressive and persistent when they realize that a whole pack of vampires is traveling together than when a lone vampire is traveling by himself. On top of that, Conrad's emotional distance from such things as his conscience and his humanity might grate on the nerves of more refined or humane Kindred, making the trip that much more tense.

• One night while Conrad is taking in the sights in a city that's technically another vampire's domain, a gang of mortal thugs steals his Pace Arrow. He gets a decent look at some of them, but he's unable to stop them from speeding away in his haven with a kidnapped woman in the back who was supposed to be his dinner the next evening. Desperate and out of options, he hands himself over to the first Kindred he can find (i.e., one or more of the players' characters) and asks for the character's help. He explains who he is and what he was doing in the domain, and he makes no secret of what the consequences could be when the thieves find his dinner in the back of the Pace Arrow. Although he can offer them nothing in return, Conrad urges his unwilling hosts to help him for the sake of preserving the Masquerade. Should one of the players' characters talk to his police or underworld contacts to try to figure out if any career criminals match the description Conrad has given him, he will discover that the Pace Arrow has already been turned over to the cops with the dead woman in the back.

Zatopek Farms

Mother is warm soil. It is the rich peat moss, shiny with moisture, but which never absorbs water. It is deep black and fertile, and it smells distantly of cow pastures and stables. It lodges under and around the edge of your fingernails, and it smells like the decaying forest floor when you bring it to your nose. Mother is a bed of dirt and worms, welcoming you back into the womb. Mother was your first home.

The Czech Tzimisce Ilya Zatopek is truly a night crawler. Robbed of memories from his mortal years, he awoke as a babe in the black soil and broke free to the surface. He remembers crawling free of the warm black womb, but nothing of the living years that preceded his Embrace and organic birth. He recalls only the pregnant European earth filled with worms… the hungry worms that ate his memories.

Resident

Deep in a part of Detroit where no children dare to play rests a rusted, ramshackle and mostly abandoned industrial park. The weed-cracked pavement of the streets passes mile after mile of sagging, rusted chain-link fence, empty, unlined parking lots, broken-down factories and skeletal warehouses. It is a reminder of this neighborhood's failed captains of industry and a shadow of yesteryear that now stains the city and refuses to wash away. Perhaps it is not surprising, then, that this section of town provides a haven for a creature as soulless as the many broken windows and abandoned buildings. Perhaps it is stereotypically baroque to find a haven here, given the fact that the industrial park is forlorn enough to suit the sensibilities of creatures living all the clichés. What is unexpected, however, is that the industrial park is actually home to a fecund, hidden environment that teems with life and growth.

Among the mess of concrete forts and age-dulled steel rests a reconverted factory that's been happily named Zatopek Farms. From the outside, the building appears to be just like any other factory. Inside, however, the high-ceilinged factory floor is a story deep in rich Czech peat moss, European night crawlers and red wigglers. The managers and employees run an unlikely and lucrative business of selling worms across North America for garbage composting, as commercial fishing bait and as high-grade reptilian/ fish/ bird feed for zoos.

As the name implies, Ilya Zatopek, now a few centuries wiser, owns this unique and thriving enterprise. A Tzimisce of the Old Country and a member of the Oradea League, he hid in the shadows of Communist Russia while fellow Fiends such as Krezhinsky and Darvag played mortal games of power and manipulation against the Ventrue. For Ilya, however, his foremost concern was always the worms. He felt closer to these burrowing organisms than he did to his own kind, and certainly more than he ever did to humankind. He raised the worms and became intimately familiar with their needs while selling them to the Russian government for their state farms (even though he figured that a fair share found its way into the Gulag diet). This is how he made a name for his enterprise in its early years.

After the Soviet Union's lumbering, staggering fall, Ilya sold his familial estates to Western entrepreneurs and even traded one small lot of land for an abandoned factory in America. Once his loyal ghouls obtained the license to import "Czech" dirt and European night crawlers into the US, both Ilya and his entourage of Oprichniki ghouls moved to their new home across the sea. His business was the first to legally offer the sale of USDA-approved European night crawlers in bulk in the US. The business was an overnight success since the four-inch invertebrates were rich in protein and instantly popular with a variety of businesses.

Currently, the Oprichniki manage the Zatopek Farms. Thanks to mail order and the Internet, nobody ever visits the factory. Therefore, the Oprichniki can work in relative seclusion, even from their innocent mortal employees. Investigators with the Department of Agriculture have visited a couple of times, but they never found anything untoward going on at the factory. Despite some unusual practices, such as filling the factory interior with earth, the business operates legally and within safety standards. Aside from the ghouls, however, no one realizes that Ilya himself is resting far beneath the soil, or that he is transforming. Unknown to everyone but his most loyal Oprichniki ghouls, he is slowly turning into a churning colony of worms.

Appearance

At the corner of two dead streets that are fast being overgrown with pernicious weeds rests the Zatopek Farms factory. The two distinct parts of the structure include the front offices and the two-and-a-half story factory building with a corrugated steel roof rising up behind it. The presence of cars in a small nearby parking lot testifies to the only signs of "life" within, while a second, larger parking lot down the street remains empty and sealed off by a chain-link fence. Behind the factory is a large driveway for trucks that leads to the docks. That too is closed off by a chain-link fence, which forces drivers to go through the front office before delivering or picking up their latest haul.

The office building is a one-story, box-like, utilitarian structure with bars across the window. Blinds remain constantly closed to prevent anyone from peeking inside. The front door window is likewise covered with blinds and inlaid with a wire mesh, but a successful Perception + Security roll (difficulty 7) reveals alarm sensors around the door and window frame. The front entrance is always locked, so visitors are granted admittance only via request through the intercom system. The alarm sounds at a nearby security firm if someone should open the door but fail to enter the proper code within 30 seconds. The alarm also sounds if someone breaks a window. The building has no motion sensors, given that someone is always moving about inside during the night or day.

The factory itself is fairly large, taking up roughly 61,000 square feet. Upon his purchase of the place, Ilya had the first-story windows bricked up and painted over, but a level-three feat of Perception allows visitors to notice a number of small exhaust ports emerging from the wall every 10 feet in a double ring around the perimeter. One set of ports is at ground level, the other set five feet above that. These openings smell strongly of fertile earth, and they are easily large enough for a rat to fit through, but they are also sealed off inside by steel mesh grating (which requires a level-five feat of Strength to bite through should a rat-sized intruder seek entry through it). Beyond this blockage is a system of fine-mesh ducts that run underneath the dirt with fans at the different junctions. This system allows the ghouls to oxygenate the deep soil regularly, while the mesh is fine enough to prevent worms of any size from passing through. It also keeps clever birds from picking off worms that stray too close to the outside.

At the rear of the factory is an elevated dock with two large garage doors, as well as an exit, all of which remain closed until someone in the front office advises shipping that visitors are en route. Otherwise, these doors will not open for anyone, regardless of who they are. After all, the ghouls have more to fear from Ilya than any stranger. The garage doors open to reveal a communal waiting area with a second set of doors standing 10 feet inside. (Without exception, truckers are not allowed to pass through these doors.) In this alcove is the shipping desk and telephone.

Layout

Almost immediately, visitors may notice that the building's interior lighting is subdued, perhaps even a few watts weak. The offices have powerful table lamps for use by management, but shadows gather in the corners like cobwebs, and everything is only a couple of shades above dark. The lack of sunlight only adds to the foreboding aspect of the place. If asked, the employees simply say that this condition is better for the worms. In truth, however, the Oprichniki abhor bright lights, much like their master. They find it more comfortable to work in semi-darkness, even though it unsettles visitors.

The offices are also a touch cooler than is entirely comfortable, a side effect from the massive air-conditioners that must always operate on the factory floor (where it is downright chilly most of the time). Again, this temperature is more conducive to worm growth, especially during the summer when temperatures soar and the building's corrugated roof amplifies the heat.

Offices

This simple office design is low on frills. The only hallway is an upside-down-L-shaped corridor with various rooms branching from it. The entryway opens into a foyer that ends at a second interior door shielded by blinds. In the foyer, a secretary's office is situated to the right behind a half-wall. Truckers and deliverymen who come to the Zatopek Farms building must wait here, and they never enter the second door (which can be opened only by a key or by the buzzer under the secretary's desk). This door is also attached to the alarm system.

Beyond the second door is a long corridor with three closed office doors on the right. To the left are one office door and two bathrooms. Offices for purchasing (supplies), accounting, orders and the offices of the president and vice-president are situated here. These rooms are all decorated solely with the lean means of business. Each office includes two chairs, a desk, a filing cabinet, a phone, a lamp, office supplies and a computer that's hooked up to the office hub. The offices lack personal touches such as photos, though there are fake potted plants here and there in the hallways as well as some posters of Eastern Europe. Otherwise there is nothing on display that would indicate the ghouls' personalities or interests.

The hallway ends at a third door with an electronic security panel on its right. The panel requires a five-digit punch code, but it can be circumvented with an Intelligence + Security roll (difficulty 6). Beyond this point lies an open room and a hallway that goes to the right. The left-hand wall has a door that connects to the factory proper, as well as a wide display window that overlooks the worm pens beyond. In front of the hallway door, along the divergent corridor, stands a set of wide windows that reveals the production manager's office.

The hallway to the right passes four tightly grouped doors on the left-hand side. The first is the aforementioned production manager's office with a large window that also overlooks the factory floor. The second door leads to a small room that serves as the office's mainframe hub, while the third opens onto a short corridor that leads to a cafeteria. The fourth office door belongs to the resident entomologist who supervises the lab. Of all the offices in the building, this last is the most distinct. Posters and diagrams of insect anatomy hang on the walls, and glass display cases of preserved specimens (some whole, some dissected) stand on the desk and cabinet top. Regardless, even this room lacks any hint of personal decoration.

At the end of the hallway is an open laboratory in which staff scientists test soil acidity and guard against protein poisoning (when the worm food decomposes and turns poisonous) and poor oxygenation. The labs also store batches of impregnated worms for later harvesting (in a refrigerated supply closet), and workers must constantly breed different species in order to generate larger worms that are less chitinous and higher in protein content. Zatopek Farms' exclusive five-inch-long night crawlers (which are much larger than the market average) are already selling out, and the harvests can barely keep up with the orders.

The cafeteria employs a private cook to handle lunches for the workers. The cafeteria also serves as the employee entrance, but the doors are open for only one hour in the morning, the lunch hour, the two half-hour breaks (in late morning and late afternoon) and a half-hour after quitting time. During these periods, an Oprichniki supervisor remains in the cafeteria to make sure that only factory workers enter or leave. Opposite the cafeteria's entrance is a third door to a small corridor that is lined with employee lockers and divided by a row of benches. Beyond that, another door, opened only at the aforementioned designated times, offers access to the factory floor in the worm pens section.

Factory Floor

The factory floor is divided into five main sections, with many portions reconverted from their former perfume and shampoo filling lines to this new enterprise. At any given time during the day, up to 50 employees might be at work harvesting worms, but Zatopek Farms rotates its staff every few months in order to keep on hand only minimum-wagers who will keep their mouths shut. Truthfully, however, the factory has a high turnover rate of mortal employees simply because the environment makes them nervous. Ilya has never fed from the workers, of course, but the Oprichniki management and austere environment set people ill at ease nonetheless. To them, the factory is a peculiar, scary place, even though they have never seen the off-limits sections that only the ghouls are allowed to tend. If the uninitiated workers were actually to see these sections, they'd probably quit that much faster.

The factory ceiling is a maze of air-conditioning ducts, water pipes and nutrient pumps (which are connected to the mixing room). The nutrient pumps link to a reinforced pipe that drops down to a 20-gallon reservoir. The reservoir connects to an array of sprayers (like pesticide sprayers) on hose tethers. This octopus-like device allows workers to move up to 20 feet away from the reservoir and still spray nutrients on the surrounding soil. Sprinklers also line the ceiling, watering certain sections twice a week with a quick spray.

Worm Pens Section

Running parallel to the office's long hallway is a large open room roughly 15,000 square feet in area. At the rear corners of the room, two parallel hallways diverge to the back of the factory, while an open archway that leads to the mixing room stands in the left-hand wall.

The worm pens are one-story, concrete, 15-foot-square towers laid out in a grid pattern in this section. The corridors that run between the numbered pens are large enough for people to walk through, despite the obstacles presented by a pair of shielded aeration ducts (five feet above one another) that runs through the pens on all four sides. To get around, workers use the grated floor that skirts the lips of the pens one story up from the ground. The grated floor is accessible via metal stairs near the connecting doors to the offices, as well as from the mixing room archway and the two corridors in the rear. The worm harvesters work on this supported landing, culling the worms at the top of the pens.

The pens also have sluice gates at the bottom. Every few weeks, the workers open the gates and drain the bottom soil into containers, dropping the pen levels by a few feet and harvesting the worms that would otherwise remain inaccessible. Workers from shipping then bring in fresh peat moss to mix with the old soil, keeping it oxygenated and fertile.

The Mixing Room

This section of the factory holds huge containers in which to mix mass batches of formulas that the staff scientists cook up in the labs. A network of pipes and hoses connects to pipes in the ceiling so that different sections can receive different nutrient formulas at the same time. Once a month, at night, the Oprichniki create a specialized batch or two consisting of a visceral soup of liquefied organs and blood, which they then spray down onto Ilya's haven. They take extra care to clean these containers afterward in order to avoid leaving evidence behind.

The Chemical Room

Situated on the ground floor of the factory, this area rests behind the worm pens, between the two corridors at the rear. Here one can find drum racks that hold various organic chemicals, as well as skids with bags of peat moss, composted fertilizer, chicken starter feed and laying mash. Additionally, the blast-proof room (normally used in businesses with volatile chemicals) was converted into a large refrigeration unit, in which workers store harvested worms that are ready for shipment. This section is open to both corridors, and it connects to the mixing room through the left-hand corridor. It connects to shipping along the right-hand corridor. As such, all three areas are devoid of ground-floor piping or ducts so that the factory forklift can move skids between shipping, mixing and the chemical rooms unimpeded.

At the back of the chemical room is a dumbwaiter-style forklift connected to the worm forest section behind the wall. Because the worm forest is on the second level, this contraption allows workers to move bulky items around without having to use the stairs.

Shipping

Shipping rests along the right-hand corridor, and it is twice as wide as its counterpart. This extra space allows the forklift to maneuver around and deliver material to the adjacent chemical room without blocking the passageway. In addition to the interior garage doors, there are three extra rooms on either side. The first is the machine shop, in which the technicians repair broken equipment. The second, larger room holds the massive air-conditioning unit, emergency generator and oxygen aeration tanks, while the third room is a small storage space for minor factory supplies (such as containers in which to ship the batches of worms).

Worm Forest

At the end of both corridors rests a metal staircase and a set of closed metal doors elevated a story-and-a-half above the ground. The doors are sealed with keys — otherwise requiring a Dexterity + Security roll (difficulty 6) to open — while the dumbwaiter's second story door can be opened only from the other side. Only the Oprichniki work here, because, as they tell people, this is where Zatopek Farms grows its greatest secret, the unique Zatopek night crawlers. In truth, though, this guarded space is Ilya's haven. At 25,000 square feet, this wide-open area is a story-and-a-half solid in rich soil. It is a plain of peat moss, unusual patches of fungal growths and Czech soil, in which Ilya can sleep comfortably.

Unlike the pens, there are no corridors here, though a large rectangular steel mesh platform is suspended a foot off the ground and runs half the room's length and width. From the doors, elevated grated walkways reach the platform. Rods from the ceiling support the entire structure and set the platform rocking a touch whenever someone walks across it. This platform is actually very safe and stable, in compliance with modern OSHA standards. Toward the head of the platform is a font that emerges from the ground through a circular hole in the mesh. Nutrient sprayers with extended hoses allow the ghouls to spray the entire area, but the font also houses the control panel for the corkscrew blades.

The room is exceedingly dark and cool, made even more so by the odd brickwork that surrounds the chamber. The unlit environment supposedly protects the worms, but it actually prevents people from taking a good look at the room. When Ilya originally moved in, he commissioned architects and an artist to turn the interior of this chamber into the likeness of a church. A character who makes a successful Perception + Alertness roll (difficulty 8) or who can see clearly in unlit conditions should notice that the platform's mesh pattern actually thickens and thins, warps and wefts to form a giant crucifix whose head ends at the font. The support rods gently curve overhead in the darkness to meet one another, forming arches like those that separate a church's nave (or central chamber) from the side arcades. In fact, the platform is symbolic of a nave, with its baptismal font emerging above the mesh cross. Anyone who succeeds on an Intelligence roll (difficulty 6) should recognize that the interior of the room bears church-like motifs, provided that person has ever been inside a church. The quarry-faced, rustic brickwork along the wall looks suspiciously like arched windows with elaborate tracery in the stonework, or Romanesque-style galleries that are slightly raised from the walls.

Ilya's body rests here, in a church of his own making. He communes with worms deep below the surface, perhaps in an effort to understand who he was before the Embrace or perhaps trying to impregnate the womb from which he himself was born. Regardless, when he manifests, he appears to be a corpse whose innards have turned into worms. He speaks while they pour over his ragged lips and out his empty eye sockets, and like a worm, he can move in and out of the earth with fluid grace.

If Ilya needs to escape his haven, he can send a portion of his body into the ductwork beneath the soil where he can pour through one section of mesh designed as his escape route. From there, he can take refuge in Worm Pen #34, which is open to the ducts and which always remains untouched. In fact, Ilya always keeps part of his mass in that pen, allowing him to eventually re-form even if 80% of his body should be destroyed (though the results of that degree of trauma remain unknown). This is fortunate, given that the worm forest has one deadly secret known only to the ghouls and Ilya.

Over half a story above the ground floor, yet still beneath the soil, are rows of corkscrew blades. Normally, the Oprichniki use the blades to rotate the earth and aerate the soil. Doing so unavoidably kills off batches of worms, but it also creates fertile ground. At higher speeds, the blades also drag topsoil down quickly, meaning that anyone caught off the platform when this happens quickly finds himself sinking in churning quicksand. If the player of such a character fails a Dexterity + Acrobatics roll (difficulty 6), the blades drag the character under and inflict 15 dice of lethal damage. Understandably, Ilya's Oprichniki ghouls never use this trick unless their master is out of the ground, or if a majority of his form has escaped into the ducts.

Story Ideas

• Seeking further enlightenment on the Path of Metamorphosis, a Sabbat Tzimisce's mentor sends him to visit Ilya at Zatopek Farms and recommends that his packmates accompany him (both for safety's sake, and on the off chance that they'll learn something). Ilya's most knowledgeable ghouls give the characters a tour and allow them to help out at feeding time, but Ilya offers little wisdom about the Path of Metamorphosis. He suggests, however, that they might gain some insight into how far he's come if they can piece together who he was before his Embrace.

• Over a few months' time, Ilya develops a powerful, unidentifiable obsession that he eventually recognizes as an illicit blood bond. Having willingly shared blood with no vampire in that period of time, however, Ilya suspects that one of his ghouls has somehow fallen under another Cainite's sway and betrayed him by mixing in an outsider's vitae with his monthly meals. He enlists the characters' help in uncovering the guilty parties and determining the motives behind the underhanded attack.

• Acting on an anonymous tip that Zatopek Farms is a front for a US-based terrorist organization and that it's producing some sort of advanced biological weaponry, a team of federal investigators closes down Zatopek Farms and begins a thorough investigation. When they manage to uncover Ilya, his Oprichniki ghouls panic and cut them off from outside contact, holding them hostage in the worm forest. The ghouls then call on the characters to help them resolve this enormous mess before it gets any more complicated. If they are able to do so, it falls to the characters to figure out who unleashed the government dogs in the first place.

The Legend of Sensual Secrets

In the realm of fantasy and empowerment, there are those who act and those who like only to watch. It seems that, in the modern nights, the latter far outweigh the former. Regardless of their reasons, some people prefer to enjoy their illicit desires at a remove, rather than engage in them directly. The proliferation of exotic dance clubs, the thriving pornographic film and print industries, the rise in theaters boasting live sex shows and even the incredible number and variety of pornographic Internet sites all testify to the fact that sometimes it's more pleasurable to look than touch.

It can be argued that this attitude mirrors the Cainite perspective on dealing with mortals vis-à-vis the Masquerade. A vampire can dwell among humans and even pretend to be one, but she is forever limited and constrained by the differences between herself and the living. Some vampires despair at those differences, becoming more and more withdrawn until the differences are so exaggerated as to be irreversible. Some, however, refuse to be entirely separated, and they crave intimate human contact. One in particular, a Brujah who goes by the name Miss Tara Sunshine, tries to draw out the most base and lascivious impulses in human beings just to remind herself what it was like to feel passionate and alive. She wants to learn all over again what it was like to be human, but like so many before her, she just wants to watch.

Resident

The Brujah who calls herself Miss Tara Sunshine used to be a plain, sexually repressed young woman named Tabitha Somerset. She grew up in Victorian-era New England, never having much of a fantasy life and never exploring much of the world beyond the walls of her father's estate. She expected either to marry and move away, or to stay behind and manage the estate after her parents passed on and her three sisters had married and left. Frankly, she didn't especially care which fate she met.

That changed, however, when a troupe of actors showed up at her father's house one evening to solicit his patronage for a new play they hoped to put on. Her father arranged a private performance for himself and several of his society friends by way of a tryout, and Tabitha decided on a whim to steal away and see the show herself. The performance that night was a suggestive, lurid and seamy affair that shocked and appalled most of the older audience members, but Tabitha was intrigued.

She followed the actors to their hotel to talk to them, ended up falling under the spell of the lead actor's powerful erotic charms and agreed that same night to leave with them and become one of the troupe. After less than a week of traveling with the actors, she discovered what they really were when the lead actor revealed his Kindred ancestry and Embraced her into his brood as he had the others. That act unlocked all the years of repressed curiosity and passion that the troupe's first performance had touched on, and Tabitha became a different creature entirely. Adopting the stage name "Miss Tara Sunshine," she reveled in her power and newfound predatory allure, and she threw herself into her performances with a zeal that impressed her sire and older broodmates. The troupe traveled up and down the East Coast performing, hunting and hiding out from more powerful vampires who didn't appreciate the troupe's occasional intrusions into their domains.

Yet, in time, even Miss Tara's passions cooled as the novelty of what she'd gotten herself into slowly faded and the reality of what she had become sank in. Spending her nights taunting and tempting audiences of spoiled humans and desperate neonates grew tedious through repetition, and her performances suffered for it. Finally, she drifted away from the troupe and settled in Florida, which was outside the troupe's usual touring range. Yet, the nights alone, shut up in rented rooms, emerging only to hunt, reminded her too much of the life she had abandoned in New England. The droning boredom was unbearably tiresome, but she no longer had the drive or energy to seek out new ways to alleviate it.

Finally, she hit upon a solution. If she couldn't manufacture and enjoy a fantasy life of her own, she would learn to appreciate those of others vicariously. She would design a place to which others could come and live out their forbidden dreams, and she would watch and experience them like the parasite she'd become. Parlaying her moderate celebrity among the eastern Camarilla Kindred she'd entertained over the years into a string of favors and donations, she bought and refurbished the house that is now her haven and private emotional playground. On paper, the establishment known as The Legend of Sensual Secrets is a decades-old acting school and private modeling agency, but in reality, it's much more.

Appearance

Tampa, Florida, where Miss Tara set up shop, is perhaps one of the most blatant examples of socio-economic dichotomy that exists in the Sunshine State gateway to the American Riviera. One might even say, as many have before, that Tampa is the dark reflection of Orlando, her pastel flamingo-pink sister to the east. If Orlando is the Mecca of the vacationing American's dreams or the bright, shining beacon of freedom from the grind of corporate Americana, then Tampa is the shadow that beacon casts.

While Orlando might be the vacation spot for millions of American families every year — and, in many cases, all year round for families who migrate there from all over the world — Tampa is the playground and amusement park of the single adult. As such, it is just as good at attracting just as many patrons for its own, special type of "entertainment." Tampa has been called the titty-bar capital of the world, boasting more fully nude adult entertainment-based establishments per city block than restaurants. While the Tampa City Council has made a concerted effort to curtail the ability of such establishments to operate within the city limits, these businesses — and the women they employ — generate a healthy chunk of Tampa's revenue nonetheless. Tampa has come to be considered a bit of a hot spot among those who travel across the countryside like moths drawn to bigger and brighter flames made of red, flickering neon lights and the overwhelmingly hypnotic thump and repetition of house music.

In the heart of the city of Tampa, just down the street from the grand, taxpayer-subsidized super stadium, lies Drew Park. This seedy, semi-industrial neighborhood is the workplace of scores of women, and the haunt of many under- and oversexed men (not to mention most of the city's sexual deviants and predators). A mere mile away from the stadium's waving princess palms and the oppressively cheerful veneer of expansive glass and blinding, shining chrome is a dark and depressing subculture draped in a facade of mystery, fantasy and sex. In actuality, the thriving Drew Park subculture is a trap that seduces women into bargaining away their youth and beauty, then tricks the sex-starved or obsessed into buying an empty promise. It is an industry built on unreality and the willingness of those involved to overlook that fact.

All the bars in the area have poorly lit parking lots, and a forest of faded signs boasts names such as "Tight Ends" or "Puss & Boots." On most windows, failing neon lights advertise cheap, domestic beer. Scantily clad waitresses who are only attractive in equally scant light serve watered-down drinks, and some are rumored to provide a more personal sort of entertainment if the price is right. Usually such women are former employees of strip clubs, lingerie shops or escort services who were rejected due to wear and tear. Many do this sort of work (with no hope of advancement and dangerously little job security) because they can't think of another way to keep from having to peddle themselves on the street.

Every other block sports X-rated video stores with every sex toy a person could imagine, and a few that should have stayed locked securely away in the recesses of some demented mind. Some adult toy stores even specialize in the demonstration (by a model of the customer's choice) of any toy he might want to purchase. Such a demonstration costs extra, of course, and most such shops require the customer to buy the item first.

There is, however, no reason for those of lesser means to despair. Drew Park has something for everyone, even those who have little to spend. For a patron who's able to see to his own needs quickly, a mere dollar or two will provide a quick fix in any of the many video arcades or peep shows that pepper the area like chicken pox. Behind fraying red drapes in decaying old shotgun houses are rows of plywood booths painted over with the same industrial grade black latex paint every other month to cover the stains and mask the smell. It is hardly attractive, but the folks who patronize such places never seem deterred. In some cases, one might even get the impression that the dank and moldy ambiance of these places adds to the level of excitement.

On the opposite end of the spectrum is The Legend of Sensual Secrets. Miss Tara Sunshine's establishment is the place of employment that could be considered the aspiration of all the aged and defeated women who are now relegated to running the beer tub at Puss & Boots (between jaunts out to the parking lot to give $25 hand jobs, that is).

Situated in the middle of a block across from the offices for a towing company and its symbiotic auto body shop is a modest-looking house with a sweeping driveway and a small, tasteful sign painted on the window of the front door which reads, "The Legend of Sensual Secrets." Most people who know of the place find its given name a bit of a mouthful. Those who know what purpose it serves call it simply The Legend.

The front of the house looks deceptively like a modest two-story private home. The grass is neatly trimmed and raked of leaves. The metal lids of the discreet sunken trashcans are painted the same color as the grass, and stick-on deodorizers inside battle the smell of the garbage. Boxes for the mail and the newspaper are dent- and rust-free, and the numbers on the wooden post that holds them up are always polished. The driveway that leads around behind the house is smooth and white thanks to regular pressure-washing, and no cracks in its surface or weeds in the seams mar it. A dark-stained, seven-foot wooden privacy fence runs flush with the front edge of the house and encircles the rear of the property. The only break in it is the double gate with polished wrought-iron fixtures.

The house itself stands out from the surrounding buildings only because it is clean and in good condition. Its two stories are paneled in sturdy aluminum siding painted a deep, unreflective brown that mimics wood grain at a distance. The windows, four-paned dark rectangles, are always unbroken and clean, flanked by decorative wooden shutters. The roof is steeply pitched, and it appears to have been re-shingled recently. The front of the house is dominated by a wooden porch and awning flanked by well-trimmed holly bushes that are surrounded in pine straw and bordered by dark, subdued railroad cross ties. Potted philodendrons hang on opposite ends of the awning. The door is heavy oak with a brass knocker, and a second wood-framed glass door, on which the name of Miss Tara's business has been stenciled in gilt paint, stands in front of it.

An astute person, however, might notice that no light shines through any of the windows. The windows, in fact, have been tinted heavily and paneled from the inside with hurricane-proof aluminum shutters that are always locked. Another indicator that this is not actually a private residence is the fact that the driveway does not lead to the garage door, but instead winds around to the back of the house and an unpaved parking lot. The wall over what was once the garage door has been firmed up with concrete-filled cinderblocks and covered with staid brown paneling that matches the rest of the house.

Layout

Even having noticed how well-kept the house looks from the outside, first-time visitors to The Legend are usually struck by the contrast between the somewhat run-down surrounding neighborhood and the elegance inside the building. Oriental rugs and masculine-looking leather furniture that would be typical of a more respectable establishment decorate the wood-paneled foyer. A giant desk of dark cherry wood sits at the far end of the room in a corner facing the door. Add a few portraits of stodgy old men hanging on the walls and a lingering odor of cigar smoke, and the foyer could be a replica of any law office or upscale social club in the country. Gilt-framed portraits do grace the walls, but not of stodgy old men; instead, they are paintings of all the stunning young women who are currently employed at The Legend. All of these women serve Miss Tara Sunshine, as the greeter at the door will quickly point out to a new visitor, and all are available to fulfill the private fantasies of those who dare to realize them.

Most new clients receive a tour of The Legend's facilities before committing to a session, and many regulars take the tour again and again in order to appreciate the variety of what The Legend has to offer. During this time they can talk in veiled terms about price and expectation. The greeter also explains to a newcomer at this point just what The Legend and its girls are there for.

Primarily, The Legend is a place in which clients can explore their fantasies. A number of theme rooms have been set up throughout the house in which clients can lose themselves for a while by indulging in a flight of fancy. Thanks to the tireless efforts of a group of stage designers whom Miss Tara keeps on retainer, the rooms simulate exotic locales or bygone eras that appeal to the imaginations of the clients. The girls who work at The Legend are skilled, well-educated actresses, trained and encouraged to find their customers' deepest hidden fantasies and act them out. Doing so sometimes involves having sex with the customers, but the girls let things go that far only if the customer has already discussed the subject with the greeter and paid a much more exorbitant fee in advance. Most of the time, the girl or girls of the customer's choice act out some prescribed interactive routine for (or with) the customer in keeping with the theme of the chosen room, and the customer takes care of business personally.

The only entrance into The Legend is the front door, which opens into the front seating room. That room connects to a hallway that leads to a stairway going up and a door that leads down into the basement. The top of the stairway between the first and second floors opens into another hallway that ends in a gilt-flecked mirrored wall. In the middle of the upstairs hallway is a trap door in the ceiling that folds down into a set of steps to the attic. The floors are covered in soft, dark brown carpets that match the doors into the theme rooms and the trim at the edges of the floors and ceilings. The walls are covered in thin brown paneling, and translucent glass fixtures overhead cast a warm, diffuse light that mutes all the edges and makes visitors feel more comfortable.

Comparing the thinness of hallways on each floor and the relatively small number of doors on each hallway to the apparent size of the house from the outside, the inside of The Legend seems somewhat smaller and more cramped than it should. This design, however, allows for the rooms themselves to be larger and to support walk-in closets full of props, costumes and makeup that allow the girls to become one with the rooms' themes. Once the client has entered the room of his choice, he is made to feel as if he's entered another world.

The Ground Floor

The first room off the greeter's room is the video room. This smallish chamber holds a leather chaise lounge and a high-definition television set equipped with a surround-sound system. Here, the greeter shows first-time clients short video clips of each of the girls who work at The Legend and are available at the moment. She follows that up with another round of pictures of each of the theme rooms so that the client knows what his options are. The client can then choose what girl (or girls) he would like to be entertained by and which room he'd like to use. He can also take a walking tour of the rest of the rooms if he's so inclined, but he doesn't get to meet the girls in person until it's time for his session to begin.

As the greeter leaves to make the necessary arrangements, the client can work up his courage (or try to find it) while he waits by watching one of dozens of pornographic vignettes programmed into the television's memory. The vignettes range from amateur to professional acting jobs, and they include lewd animated shorts of all varieties. If the client is particularly low on funds (or simply a coward), he can spend an hour in this room paging through the recorded scenes, then pay the greeter a greatly reduced (although not insignificant) fee. First-time clients who do so, however, are not usually allowed back into The Legend.

The Bathing Room

The first theme room downstairs is the Bathing Room, essentially nothing more than a bathroom with an ornate shower and a huge tub. The shower is a tiled enclosure large enough for four people to stand, kneel or even lie down in. The bathtub is an equally large black porcelain basin with whirlpool jets all around and a small, raised stand in the middle. The fixtures are gold-plated chrome, and two black-lacquered cabinets stand on either side of the mirror on the wall left of the door. These cabinets hide a modest stereo system and hold an array of bath items from imported bath salts to sea sponges to fluffy towels to large bathrobes with the word Legend embroidered on the cuffs. In the corner by the door is a squat, enameled bench that the client can either sit on to watch the girls work or leave his clothes folded on top of if he wants to get involved himself.

The Locker Room

The next theme room is designed like a girl's high-school locker room. Two rows of lockers face each other, and a long wooden bench runs between them. On the back wall is a long Formica counter with two sinks and a wall mirror. The locker doors are decorated with pictures of teen idols and hand-painted graffiti, and none of them are locked. Most of the lockers are even stocked with ladies' clothes, as if their owners are in gym class and the client has just snuck in unnoticed. If a client looks long enough, he might even find a diary full of lurid teenage-girl fantasies or some sex toy that a high-school girl might conceivably sneak into a school for the thrill of doing something against the rules.

Some clients go into this room just for the thrill of sneaking around somewhere they wouldn't be allowed in, and they don't involve any of Miss Tara's girls. Most, however, pick one or more of the younger-looking girls to act out a scene. The girls might treat the client like he's invisible by undressing and then either masturbating or experimenting with each other sexually as if the client isn't in the room. Or the girl(s) might "catch" the client "sneaking around" and playfully "punish" him for being so naughty.

The other rooms on the first floor are off-limits to guests. They include a kitchen, a bathroom/dressing room for the girls and a meeting room with a circular table and a ring of chairs.

Upstairs

Sessions in the rooms upstairs are a little more expensive, but those rooms are somewhat more elaborately decorated, and they offer fantasies that are a little more complex.

The Honeymoon Suite

The first such room is made up to look like a gaudy honeymoon suite in a hotel. It's decorated in whites, pinks and reds, and the wallpaper is an alternating red and pink stripe pattern trimmed in white hearts. The bed is a circular apparatus with heart-shaped pillows and a large red heart in the center of the bedspread. It's accented by a semicircle of velvet curtains, and it can be made to heat up, vibrate or turn slowly at the touch of a button set on the wall behind it. The cushions and filigree of the chairs around the room all keep with the heart motif, and the loveseat against the wall is nothing more than a giant corduroy-upholstered heart with arms. Even the wall mirror, which hangs over a mini wet-bar, is cut in the shape of two hearts side by side with two acid-etched cupids shooting arrows at each other on either side. All in all, the room is pretty tacky and silly-looking, but its kitschy, saccharine aspect appeals to some of the customers' ironic sense of humor.

In the closet hang several outfits of various sizes, all of which are designed to add to the client's role-playing experience. They include black tuxedoes, bright white gowns, room service liveries, hotel robes and saucy-maid outfits. When a client's time in this room is over, a white French phone on the heart-shaped night table rings and delivers the message. Should the client turn on the 17" black-and-white television that sits on a white night table opposite the closet, a taped graphic reading "Welcome Newlyweds" alternates with a five-day weather report forecasting constant rain.

The Oriental Den

The next room is decorated in the style of a fantastically exaggerated Chinese opium den. A tall jade-inlaid brass hookah pipe with half a dozen hoses around the base dominates the center of the room and stands four feet tall. There's no actual opium in it, but an additional fee can see it supplied with high-quality marijuana if the client's interested. Otherwise, it simply burns incense.

Bronze Buddha statuettes lounge in the corners, and silk paintings of Chinese landscapes and ornate monasteries hang on the walls. Standing beneath one large landscape, a long, thin aquarium full of angelfish burbles away quietly. Velvet and silk cushions are scattered around the floor, and the client is encouraged to fill the room with as many of Miss Tara's girls as he can afford. He can then sit in the large wooden throne on a raised dais behind the hookah pipe opposite the door and command the girls to do whatever he wants. On the wall behind the throne is a mural of a coiled, Oriental dragon that appears to be looking over the shoulder of whoever's in the chair. The dragon is painted in iridescent green, red and gold, and four small blacklights hidden behind silk drapings make its scales glow. Two small mirrors take the place of the dragon's eyes, so that the client can look in them and see only himself.

The Jail Cell

The last theme room on this floor is decorated to look like a modern jail cell. The client comes in through the hallway door to find a second wall of iron bars a few feet ahead with an open cell door at one end. Inside the cell are two bunked cots, metal frames bolted to the wall and secured by heavy chains. The dingy, sagging mattresses are covered in rough gray wool blankets, and a single blue-pinstriped pillow rests at the head of each. The cell has a lidless metal toilet at the end opposite the gate, next to which is an empty metal shelf beneath a one-foot-square wall mirror. A single light hangs overhead in a wire cage, operated by a switch next to the door of the room.

In this room, the client can pretend to be an inmate in a male prison with only female guards. He could also be the warden (or guard) at an all-female prison who's bartering with a desperate woman for an early release. A popular fantasy is that of the death-row inmate who receives an "unexpected" visitor delivering his last meal. If he so chooses, the client can even act as an invisible spectator, watching as two female inmates get intimately acquainted after lights-out.

On this floor, one can also find a prop closet, a half bathroom for guests and a spare, unadorned bedroom that the girls are allowed to stay in if they can't go home when their work shift is over.

The Attic

The attic of The Legend has only recently been converted into a space for entertaining customers. It was originally divided into a small bedroom and an unfinished storage space. Since Miss Tara had it renovated, the exposed beams and puffy pink insulation have been covered by a sturdy plywood floor, and more vents have been cut into the roof to keep it from becoming too stuffy in the summer.

The Tent

Thick, expensive fabric has been draped from the ceiling in the old storage area to create the illusion of being inside a luxurious tent fit for a sheik. Moroccan carpets and brass incense burners set on finely carved black tables are accentuated by muted red lights. The client is provided with loose cotton robes and other apparel in which to dress to make himself feel like Laurence of Arabia, and the employees are more than happy to act the part of willing harem girls in fine golden chains and mysterious silk veils. The client will also find an old, graphically illustrated copy of *Arabian Nights* on a small table in the back of the tent if he's absolutely stuck for lascivious inspiration.

The Dressing Room

The former bedroom has been converted into a dressing room, and it usually appeals to clients who wish to pretend to be something they are not. A walnut vanity and stool, two enormous bureaus and a hinged department store fitting-room mirror are the only pieces of furniture in the room. It also holds a moderate closet full of costumes and shoes of all styles and sizes. The basic idea behind the room is for the client to go inside with at least two girls (but no more than three) and choose what sort of outfit he wants to see them in. The girls then dress and undress each other as the client directs. Sometimes a client also has the girls dress and undress him in ways he'd never look in public or even try out in the privacy of his home. Many clients spend a session in this room getting into costume (and character) for a session in one of the theme rooms, but some are content to spend the entire time in here playing make-believe.

The Basement

At the bottom of the carpeted steps leading down from the hallway above is another shorter hallway between four rooms. This hallway is lit by a single bulb on a chain, its bare concrete floor partly covered with cheap tan carpet. The doors on either side of the hall closest to the steps are rough, unfinished wood of the same make as those upstairs. Another door, made of thick oak, stands at the far end of the hall. No keyhole is visible from the outside, but it remains firmly locked from the inside. At a right angle to that door is a thinner door with no lock whatsoever. That door leads into an uncarpeted room with bare studs for a ceiling and blank cinderblocks for a back wall. Inside this room is the water-heater, a stacked washer-dryer unit and a run-of-the-mill electricity generator to prevent blackouts.

Clients are only taken to the two rooms closest to the steps when they come downstairs. While not the most expensive rooms inside The Legend, they are certainly two of the most interesting. Because of what goes on in these rooms, hidden baffles have been built into the walls and ceilings so as to trap the sounds of the clients carrying on inside.

The Ring

The first room is known as the Ring, and its function is exactly what the name implies. In the middle of the room is a raised and roped-off square built to the specifications of a regulation boxing ring. A set of hollow metal steps leads up into the ring, and wooden stools stand outside at two of the opposing corners. A pair of metal cabinets holds an array of workout clothes and a selection of boxing gear (from two-pound gloves to mouthpieces to padded helmets to foot pads) in red and blue. One can even find such unusual items as weighted jump-ropes, colorful luchador masks and boxing trainer punching pads with worn-out pictures of Fidel Castro and Saddam Hussein on them.

A bright blue-white stage light hangs overhead to cast a glare on the ring, which makes it a little hard to see the walls clearly from the middle of the room. This effect is deliberate, because the walls are painted to resemble a crowded boxing (or professional wrestling) arena. They have been primed in basic black, with the vague, colorful shapes of spectators painted on top of that. The shapes diminish in size and distinction the closer they are to the ceiling, and small blue lights have been rigged among them to flash intermittently, simulating camera flash bulbs. The room even has a stereo system that can be cued to play the sounds of a crowd cheering on the client as he wrestles or boxes against one of the girls, plays referee between two girls as they have it out, puts one of the girls through a rigorous training regimen or has one of the girls do so for him.

The Dungeon

The last theme room is, by far, the most interesting one. Its walls, floor and ceiling are all gray faux stone, and its "furniture" is all macabre black wood. Standing on their own or set up on wooden tables and benches around the room is a full complement of authentically replicated Inquisition-era torture devices. These devices range from simple thumbscrews to a working rack to a pillory to a trick iron maiden. The room even has a fake guillotine and a recently added mockup of an electric chair. The blade of the guillotine stops inches before it hits the victim's neck, and the electric chair is nothing more than a flashy, sinister-looking gizmo with some strategically placed metal plates that vibrate at a high frequency when the "torturer" throws the switch. In fact, each of the torture devices is equipped with clutches, breakaway harnesses and mechanical stops to ensure the safety of whoever is using them. On top of that, each of the girls in Miss Tara's employ has been trained to operate the machines and to show clients how to operate them. The thrill of acting out fantasies in this room comes from the girls' ability to act like they're being tortured, then regroup and beg the customer for more.

The Reality Behind the Fantasy

As elegant as an experience in one of the rooms might sound to a potential customer, the constant reminders of who a client is and where he is are difficult to banish. In every room, one can find plain, white hand towels, bottles of Astroglide, condoms and a dispenser of baby wipes, which all happen to be strategically placed for ease of access. When the fantasies are all over and the girl or girls of the client's choice have fulfilled his desires, the girls who were not selected by any client that day enter the room with a pair of latex gloves, spray disinfectant and disposable terrycloth towels to clean up any residual mess. In many cases, what gets thrown out in the garbage on any given night is the only thing left of the fantasies made flesh within the walls of The Legend.

Miss Tara's Haven

The final room in the basement is both different from and similar to each of the other rooms in the house. It is completely unadorned and sparsely furnished. The walls are all concrete-filled cinderblock covered in white latex paint. A single cot without blankets or a pillow lies in the corner, a US Army footlocker full of blue jeans and sweatshirts sits at the end of it, and a large metal desk stands opposite it.

The desk's drawers hold The Legend's financial records, and two expensive personal computers sit on top of it. The overhead lights are simple fluorescent bulbs in a workman-like rectangular fixture. The only concession to decoration is the high-backed leather chair at the desk, which rocks and swivels at the base. A tangle of wires runs down from the ceiling into the backs of the computers, and the computers themselves are plugged into a surge-protector power strip on the floor. A combination phone/intercom sits on the desk next to the computers.

Its lack of adornment makes this room unlike most of the others in the house, but like them, it is a den of fantasy and self-delusion. Here Miss Tara sits every night arranging entertainment for her clients, managing business affairs, spying on her customers and trying to re-experience her lost passions through the acts they carry out with her girls. She spies on her customers using her computers, which are connected to miniature digital cameras tucked away inside each of her theme rooms. Most of them are positioned in alcoves behind strategically placed two-way mirrors; those in rooms that have no mirrors are hidden either in darkened corners or behind particularly bright lights that disguise them with glare.

Down here Miss Tara pays her bills, returns phone calls after dark, evaluates her girls' recorded performances and feeds. When she's not performing any of those activities (or watching live as some customer acts out a fantasy), she's watching her favorite previously recorded acts on the computer and trying to figure out what she's missing in all this fun that her customers seem to be having.

SECURITY

Security at The Legend is a fairly simple affair. The foremost tactic in keeping the place safe is not to advertise its existence too openly. Miss Tara's girls spread the word only seldom, and the only advertisement in print is the white-pages listing for "Sunshine, Tara" in the phone book. Word usually gets around about The Legend through satisfied customers. Since most such customers have a vested interest in *not* letting their colleagues or immediate family know where they've been spending so much time and money, however, such word of mouth spreads slowly.

Physical security measures are minimal as well. The deeply tinted windows have all been locked, nailed shut and sealed with paint from the inside, and heavy aluminum hurricane shutters have been affixed inside as well. The windows inside each of the theme rooms have been further camouflaged by the addition of false walls that isolate the clients from the "real" world outside. There's only one door into the building, the heavy oak front door that's double-bolted and chained shut during the day while the place is closed.

Miss Tara's personal room in the basement is equally fortified with cinderblock walls and the bare concrete of the foundation for a floor. Her door is heavy oak like the house's front door, with a push-button thumb lock on the doorknob and a deadbolt on either side of it. Since the deadbolts have no exterior keyholes and the hinges are hidden inside the doorframe, a determined intruder would have to chop the door down with a fire ax to get inside. In fact, a determined intruder might have just as much luck battering his way through the room's wooden ceiling from the floor of the kitchen upstairs. Either such rash, brutal act, however, would likely make enough noise and take enough time to wake the sleeping undead resident within.

MISS TARA'S GIRLS

A final note of consideration must be given to the girls in Miss Tara's employ. Every single one of them is a vibrant, nubile young woman of a different ethnicity than her coworkers, and none of them has any shame about doing exactly what their customers want. They're all trained in makeup, acting, costuming and even a little set design, and they command a pool of abilities between them that ranges from carpentry to gourmet cooking to financial planning to computer programming to advanced first aid.

Back when she was still designing The Legend of Sensual Secrets, Miss Tara sought each of her girls out individually from acting troupes, modeling agencies, schools of performing arts, strip clubs and even a high school in one instance. She used hypnotic Presence charms and subtle means of blood-bonding over several weeks apiece to seduce the girls into coming to work for her. She has since trained them to be loyal and valuable ghouls, as well as borderline blood dolls from whom she can feed without having to go to the trouble of hunting all the time.

Thoroughly addicted to her blood and the ecstatic agony of the Kiss, the girls will do anything for Miss Tara. In fact, they get so deeply into the performances they put on for clients because they know Miss Tara is watching them and counting on them to stir up the passions she so desperately misses. The promise of eternal beauty, youth and vigorous life (not to mention the enormous paychecks they get from Miss Tara every week) are all just bonuses in the package.

STORY IDEAS

• Random allies, contacts or even ghouls of the players' characters begin making frequent, illicit trips to The Legend and engaging in the worst sort of aberrant sexual behavior with Miss Tara's girls. Knowing who these clients represent, Miss Tara threatens to expose them unless the members of the coterie to whom they are attached start doing favors for her or supporting her in front of the local Kindred authorities. Mired in a conflict of interests, the coterie members must go to The Legend themselves and try to reason with Miss Tara.

• Miss Tara awakes late one evening to find The Legend swarming with police and surrounded by television crews. One of her girls, it seems, has been savagely beaten to death, and her review of the spy camera footage for earlier that day reveals that the culprit was a notorious witch-hunter. She calls upon allies (i.e., the players' characters) in town to help her squelch any potential breach in the Masquerade and track down the killer who invaded her home before he returns to finish the job.

• Three of Miss Tara's girls show up late for work one night, and when they finally appear, they've all been Embraced. Acting on some bizarre (seemingly programmed) impulse, the three of them fall on each of the others and Embrace them all as Miss Tara watches in dumbfounded horror. Between them, they tear apart The Legend's two clients for the evening, then come downstairs and make every effort to get into Miss Tara's locked room. Miss Tara is able to make a desperate call for help before two of the girls start throwing switches in the fuse box and turn off the electric generator. If they can make it in time, the players' characters' coterie must get to The Legend, try to get to Miss Tara before her girls do, then find out what the hell is going on and why.

• The players' characters make up a Sabbat pack that comprises one or two of the Cainites who originally seduced Tabitha Somerset and made up the troupe of actors with whom she ran away. Now, after more than a century, those Cainites have found honor and glory as part of the Sword of Caine, and they believe that "Miss Tara" would make a worthy addition to the cause. They also hope to cure her of the lingering ennui that drove her away from them to begin with. After a tour (and perhaps a sample) of what The Legend offers, the characters must try to convince Miss Tara to seek the vitality and excitement she's been missing by joining the Sabbat.

THE LEGEND OF SENSUAL SECRETS

The Venetian

In 1945, mobster Benjamin "Bugsy" Siegel came to the sleepy desert town of Las Vegas with a dream. He dreamed of turning a town that was little more than brief stopover for the Union Pacific Railroad on its way to Los Angeles into a shining oasis where Hollywood's elite would come to escape the pressures of Tinseltown for a little while. And if they dropped a load of cash at his mob-financed Flamingo Casino, there was no harm in that either….

Unfortunately for Siegel, the reality of the situation was a lot harsher than his dream. His $1.2 million sure-fire investment of mob funds ballooned into a $6 million fiasco. Siegel called in all his favors from the mob and from among his friends in Hollywood to raise the additional cash, and, just to be on the safe side, he diverted a small amount of money from construction into a numbered Swiss bank account.

That last bit was a big mistake, because the mob bosses he'd borrowed from got wind of his skimming of the construction fund. It was only "Bugsy" Siegel's long-standing friendship with mob boss Meyer Lansky that brought him a brief reprieve. If the casino turned out to be the big moneymaker Siegel promised, all would be forgiven.

Yet despite top-notch entertainment from Rose Marie, George Raft, Jimmy Durante, emcee George Jessel and Xavier Cugat's orchestra and the appearance of notable film stars such as Clark Gable, Lana Turner and Caesar Romero, the Flamingo's grand opening was a flop. The hotel was unfinished, and prospective guests were forced to return with their casino winnings to downtown hotels such as the Frontier.

Despite another reprieve lasting until the Flamingo's grand reopening in May of '47, Siegel's fate was sealed. On June 20, 1947 at approximately 10:30 PM, "Bugsy" Siegel perished in a hail of bullets fired through the living room window of his Hollywood home. But though he never lived to see it, Siegel's dream came true. The casinos of Las Vegas bring in billions of dollars of profit each year. "Bugsy" Siegel was right.

Fifty years later, someone else decided to make Las Vegas his home. He'd been there years before, back when Frankie and his Rat Pack were the talk of the town. Back when he still drew breath. Now Dante Giovanni has returned to Sin City. And just like "Bugsy" Siegel before him, he, too, has a dream.

Resident

Born in 1903, Dante Giovanni Putanesca came from a dirt-poor family, and he himself was only moderately literate. Not wanting to end up a loser like his alcoholic father, Dante turned to one of the few lucrative avenues of employment available to someone of his background in the 1920s on Chicago's South Side — organized crime.

Not long after he made that decision, Dante came to the attention of his "great-uncle," Lorenzo Putanesca, who was then visiting Chicago from the old country. Lorenzo was deeply disappointed by the sorry state of the family in America. However, in Dante, Lorenzo saw a spark of dark and terrible potential, enough that he was willing to bestow on the man the Proxy Kiss.

Soon after, Lorenzo left Chicago, having had enough of that arrogant *bucaiòlo* Lodin's attitude, and he took his young ghoul with him. The two settled in Los Angeles, whose coastal climate reminded Lorenzo of his home in Napoli. Still, despite his new duties as a ghoul, Dante was a gangster at heart, and soon fell in with the criminal element in LA. He swiftly discovered that gangsters were chic with the Hollywood crowd, so he began to attend all the gala premieres, the happening parties and the industry award shows, which was fine with Dante's domitor as it netted him more influence in the film industry. While hanging with the Hollywood in crowd, Dante met another infamous mobster, Benny Siegel.

The two men became fast friends, which is not unusual considering how much they had in common. Both enjoyed the company of beautiful women and living the lifestyle of a movie star. And even though both men possessed hair-trigger tempers, ready to explode at the slightest provocation, they got along famously. It was not surprising, therefore, that Siegel approached Dante for additional funds when the money to finance his dream ran out. Dante became fascinated by the potential of the Flamingo and convinced Lorenzo to help pony up the million-plus dollars in cash needed to complete construction.

Unfortunately, the Flamingo's opening was a bust, and the promised returns on the Cainite's investment did not immediately come rolling in. This state of affairs was inexcusable to a frugal vampire such as Lorenzo, so Lorenzo refused to let Dante intervene when sentence was passed on his friend Benjamin. Lorenzo didn't even let Dante have the dignity of pulling the trigger himself, but he made sure that Dante was well aware of the price of failing his new masters. Luckily for Dante, the Flamingo finally turned a profit around the same time Siegel was murdered, validating the ghoul's belief in the casino's viability.

Pleased with his ghoul's performance (and obedience), Lorenzo expanded Dante's duties to include overseeing the vampire's investment in the Flamingo. Through much of the late '40s and the 1950s, Dante made frequent trips back and forth between Los Angeles and Las Vegas. In that time, he became enamored of the Vegas nightlife — the lights, the gambling, the showgirls, the Rat Pack — and decided that, if he was ever Embraced by his domitor, he would make a home for himself in Las Vegas.

Such was not to be, however, as the influx of tourists and money to Las Vegas had already lured vampires to the city by the mid-50s. These vampires, including the new prince, rapidly consolidated their hold over the city, and Dante was forced to surrender his, and his master's, influence over the Flamingo by the early '60s. Still, the casino's profits had more than made up for Lorenzo's initial investment by that time, so Dante was not punished for his failure to hold onto the Flamingo. Instead, Lorenzo rewarded Dante for his shrewdness in convincing him to invest in such an unorthodox venture by Embracing him.

In the early 1980s, Dante left LA to strike out on his own. Since then, he has operated for a time in several cities — Chicago, Baton Rouge, Atlanta — but his temper and his attitude always seem to get him into hot water with the powers that be. Most recently forced out of Atlanta by its war between the Sabbat and the Camarilla, Dante decided that there should be a neutral place where vampires from different sects could go and deal with one another without all the damn fire-and-stakes crap. Then he remembered how it had felt all those years ago talking to Benny about what Las Vegas was going to be, and it hit him. Why not Las Vegas?

Mustering what little influence he had within his clan, Dante presented his proposal to a coalition of Giovanni *anziani* headed by his sire. Lorenzo still harbored a soft spot for his hot-blooded childe — and he recalled how Dante had been correct about Vegas's profitability to him before — so he lent his support to the young vampire. (It probably didn't hurt matters that Shlomo Rothstein, the dominant Giovanni in Las Vegas, was the childe of a rival of Lorenzo, Julietta Putanesca, and that Dante's presence in the city, and erratic behavior, was almost certain to weaken his position as *capo*.)

The other Giovanni assented, nominally because the proposal was a sound one (at least on the surface) but also on the off chance that Dante Giovanni (embarrassing liability to the clan that he was) might finally meet his end. After all, they reasoned, if the Brujah could not protect Carthage and Michael's Dream of Constantinople could not endure, what chance did one hotheaded Giovanni have of keeping the peace between vampires who have hated one another for centuries? Then, once Dante had worked himself out of the picture, they could turn the place into a more respectable, more discreet, Giovanni investment.

Once that had been decided, the Venetian Resort Hotel Casino opened to the public on May 3, 1999, and one vampire's dream came to fruition.

Appearance

The Venetian is centrally located on the infamous Vegas Strip (Las Vegas Boulevard) where it intersects with Sands Avenue, next to the Casino Royale and directly across from the Mirage. It was built on the former site of the Sands, a popular hotel and casino of the 1950s and '60s.

The Venetian is modeled on Venice, Italy, and so the exterior façade features details from that city. A moving sidewalk built to resemble Venice's Rialto Bridge crosses over an artificial canal (complete with bobbing gondolas) from the replica Campanile Tower to the Venetian proper.

To the left of the bridge lie the Ca D'Oro and the Doge's Palace. To the right rests a modern valet drop-off done up in the style of Venice and audaciously named the Porte Cochère. And rising up 35 stories from the center of this homage to Renaissance architecture is the giant Y-shaped tower of the Venetian hotel.

Layout

Built at a cost of approximately $1.4 billion, the Venetian is a masterpiece of casino design. It succeeds in bringing traditional European style and luxury to Las Vegas, featuring reproductions of Venice's finest works of art and architecture. Within the structure, Venice's Grand Canal and Saint Mark's Square have been re-created down to the finest detail.

Twelve upscale restaurants on the premises serve guests of the Venetian, including Wolfgang Puck's Postrio and Emeril Lagasse's Delmonico Steakhouse. One restaurant bears mention for more than just its cuisine, however. WB Stage 16 is a favorite haunt of Dante Giovanni. Its reproduction of the Sand's Regency Room takes him back to his breathing days and the Vegas he fell in love with. He also likes to entertain guests in the restaurant's Velvet Lounge because of the unparalleled view it offers of the Strip.

Other highlights of the Venetian include the Grand Canal Shoppes (a 500,000-square-foot, themed, indoor retail mall featuring cobbled walkways and a reproduction of Venice's Grand Canal, complete with gondolas), the Canyon Ranch SpaClub (a 65,000-square-foot "oasis of health and rejuvenation" in the form of a Venetian garden), the Guggenheim Las Vegas, Madame Tussaud's Wax Museum and entertainment in the form of the V Bar, La Scena and the Showroom at the Venetian (whose third-floor cigar and martini bars are two of Dante's other favorite hangouts).

The Hotel

The Venetian is the first all-suite hotel on the Vegas Strip, and it has 3,036 rooms. (The addition of Phase II, now under construction, will make the Venetian the largest hotel in the world.) The smallest room is the 700-square-foot Luxury Suite. From there, the suites progress from the Bella Suite to the Rialto Suite to the Piazza Suite and, finally, the Venetian's three 55,000-square-foot Presidential Suites. These suites are typically reserved for the highest of high-rollers — known as whales in casino jargon — and they are usually "comped" to said high-rollers by the management. (This practice is intended to keep the high-rollers coming back to the casino and spending huge wads of money there rather than taking their business elsewhere.) Kindred dignitaries whom Dante is trying to impress usually end up in one of these suites as well, but it's up to Dante personally to see that the management comps the suite. Anyone who actually pays a Presidential Suite's $10,000-a-night price tag who is not recognized by the management or invited to do so by Dante is sure to receive Dante's attention.

Within the corporate structure of the Venetian, Dante Giovanni acts as a Vice President of Hotel Operations. This position allows him to comp a vampiric guest with any suite he wishes. (Or not to do so, if he thinks the guest in question will be trouble.) It also gives him authority over all hotel and casino staff. If a Toreador archon wants an after-hours visit to the Bellagio Gallery of Fine Art (or even a Brujah *antitribu* to Elvis-A-Rama), Dante can have the Venetian's concierge set the vampire up.

Baggage World

When guests arrive at the Venetian hotel and check in, their luggage is shunted into tunnels that lead underground to a portion of the hotel called Baggage World. Basically, this facility allows guests' baggage to be taken up service elevators to their rooms in an effort to avoid the congestion in public areas and elevators caused by bell carts. Of course, the system also allows things to travel down from hotel rooms away from the prying eyes of the kine. In a worst-case scenario, a dead body could be smuggled out of the Venetian and down to a car with no guest ever seeing it. Just to be safe, hacksaws are to be taken to such bodies by on-site ghouls so that the parts can be bagged up and sent down in nondescript suitcases. Granted, no guest has yet relied on this grisly contingency, but Dante is eager to inform his important Kindred guests of its availability. Doing so is his way of letting his undead guests know that he's got their best interests at heart, and also an unsubtle method of fishing for material with which to blackmail his indiscreet patrons, should the opportunity arise.

The Casino

Featuring a 116,000-square-foot casino, the Venetian offers gamers, both human and Cainite, a wide variety of options. The casino's 110 table games include poker, blackjack, roulette, craps, baccarat, keno — even war. A portion of the casino's table games are devoted to traditional Asian games such as *pai gow* and were designed by the della Passaglia according to *feng shui* principles that maximize *joss* to put Asian guests' minds at ease. (Dante also figured it wouldn't hurt to have a place available for Cathayans to play, considering the inroads they've made in California, but no Cathayan in 1,000 square miles has yet deigned to come near the place.) The Venetian also has 2,500 slot machines, ranging from nickel slots all the way to 500 dollars, for players fond of these one-armed bandits. And guests who enjoy wagering on sports from football to horse races are sure to appreciate the casino's state-of-the-art race and sports lounge, where they may simultaneously place bets and watch all their favorite events on big-screen monitors.

Vampires, much like high-rollers, are offered a chance to play in private rooms away from the masses, and they are also extended membership to the Venetian's Gold Club Lounge. These are the only two places in the public areas of the casino not monitored by surveillance personnel, allowing Kindred to speak freely without fear of violating the Masquerade. All of Prince Benedic's rules regarding gambling are strictly enforced, however. Therefore, no Kindred can play poker, nor may any Kindred lose more than $10 million in a single evening.

Dante's Haven

Dante rests in a modified version of the Venetian's Piazza Suite on the 17th floor facing the Strip. The suite is 1,319 square feet in area (which is larger than many two-bedroom apartments). A set of double doors leads into the haven's entranceway of real Italian marble. During the day, these doors are locked, bolted and barred, and an electronic alarm has been installed to alert surveillance personnel (and through them, hotel security) of any attempt to force said doors open. (The electronic keypad responsible for activating and deactivating the alarm is mounted next to Dante's bed.)

The suite features a formal dining area, a sunken living room and a complete wet bar (from which Dante occasionally makes martinis that end up going to waste). He also keeps a moderate stash of Rohypanol and Percodan hidden in the bar so that he can make a loaded drink for a guest he's lured to his suite for a private snack. The living room's two windows are made of highly tinted bulletproof glass and are heavily curtained. The room contains a convertible sofa, coffee table, four upholstered chairs (two with ottomans), an entertainment center (complete with a 36" television and a combination stereo and home-theater system) and a desk with phone, laptop computer and combination fax/printer.

Dante's bedroom contains a queen-sized bed, a chaise lounge, a 27" TV in a bedroom armoire, a large closet full of designer suits, a chest of drawers and two nightstands. The double doors leading into the bedroom are locked, bolted and barred during the daytime hours just as the suite's outer doors are, and Dante rests with a silenced .45 under his pillow. Whereas the standard Piazza Suite has only a curtain separating the bedroom from the living room, Dante's has a wall in place to keep any sunlight from reaching him during the day. The suite also features a 130- square-foot bathroom finished in Italian marble. At night, however, it is unusual to find Dante in his haven. Though Dante occasionally seduces victims by luring them up to his suite, he's more likely to entertain guests or try to impress respected Kindred dignitaries in the Velvet Lounge or the Regency Room.

The Staff

The Venetian employs hundreds of team members who work at jobs ranging from pit boss to bellhop. With its competitive salaries, comprehensive health care, on-site child care and team member concierge service, the Venetian has no trouble attracting potential employees. Almost none of the resort's team members are aware of the existence of a vampire in their midst, much less that the Venetian, in addition to its usual patrons, caters to a unique clientele of undead. If anyone on staff suspects Dante Giovanni to be anything more than a secretive "Vice President of Operations," they suspect that he's a mobster. As anywhere else in Las Vegas, the Masquerade is strictly enforced among the Venetian's Kindred guests.

Security

The one section of the staff on whom Dante does keep a tight rein is security. Venetian security falls into three subsections: surveillance, uniformed officers and investigators. Surveillance is the smallest department on staff at the resort. At any given time, only two people man the Venetian's Surveillance Room, but they remain in constant contact with the uniformed officers and, when necessary, they may make contact with the undercover investigators. Surveillance coordinates the rest of the security personnel and is answerable only to the Director of Surveillance (and, through him, to his domitor, Dante Giovanni). The uniformed officers, armed with pistols and nightsticks, make up a private security force employed by the casino to maintain order. They may detain suspects for the police, but they have no actual legal authority outside the Venetian.

The investigators are plainclothes security personnel who cruise the casino looking for anything that JDLR (just doesn't look right). They also act as Dante's personal enforcers. The lead investigator and several subordinates have been ghouled by Dante, and those who aren't ghouls are, to a man, members of the Giovanni family or one of its many offshoots. Typically armed with handguns, investigators who know they are going up against vampires may have more exotic weapons on hand, such as stakes or compact cattle prods.

As an added measure of security, Dante uses members of the Sands' *spirito* population to keep him informed of the arrival of any Cainites or of anything that, to the wraiths, JDLR. Also, during the rash of vampire disappearances two years ago, Dante stationed two ghoul investigators in

The Sands

An unexpected side effect of building the Venetian on the former site of the Sands Hotel and Casino has been that the old structure still exists across the Shroud. Its ghostly architecture runs throughout the heart of the new building, giving Dante the power to travel about the Venetian's core without being observed by its patrons, be they kine or Kindred. The Sands also provides Dante with a good-sized population of *spiriti* and *spettri* to boss around, trapped as they are by the maelstrom that is currently raging throughout the Underworld.

his suite to watch over him during the day. Furthermore, Dante's Piazza Suite coincides with the location of the penthouse of the old Sands across the *Sudario*. Dante's prowess with Necromancy is such that he may step through the Shroud and use the Sands' penthouse elevator, whose physical location coincides with his bedroom, as a means of egress in case of emergency. The room beneath Dante's suite is always kept vacant in case he must do so.

The Eye in the Sky

From a small room deep within bowels of the Venetian, surveillance personnel use a system of 1,000 cameras to monitor activity within the resort. Each of these cameras is concealed by a smoked globe and may rotate 360 degrees a second, allowing patrons to be followed through the resort from the moment they enter the building to the time they reach their rooms, including in the elevators. The Venetian employs state-of-the-art facial-imaging technology, which measures the distance between a subject's eyes to match her with a database of known criminal offenders. At Dante's behest, this technology is covertly being applied to Kindred recognition as well.

Once the facial-recognition software has picked out a perpetrator or vampire, either uniformed officers, investigators or Dante himself is informed, and then appropriate action may be taken. By official order, Venetian surveillance team members are segregated from the rest of the casino personnel. They use separate entrances, and they don't fraternize with other employees. As such, and because of its usefulness, it's not surprising that the surveillance staff is completely under the influence of Dante, and the Director of Surveillance is the vampire's blood-bound ghoul.

Story Ideas

• Giovanni agents of Rothstein take it upon themselves to have Dante Giovanni get himself ousted (if not outright killed) by the Kindred authorities of Las Vegas. They incite the *spiriti* and *spettri* who have holed up in the Underworld reflection of the Sands into causing terrifying disturbances that drive off guests and push Dante into dealing with them. Working in teams to good effect, these Giovanni agents force Dante to spread himself very thin, which makes his temper flare and his sense of self-control erode. It's up to the players' characters' coterie (assuming that the players' characters are supporters of Dante's grand ideas and are not the Giovanni agents provocateurs in the first place) to keep Dante calm, clean up his messes and find out who's trying to get him in trouble.

• Accepting Dante's standing (but unspoken) invitation to come and enjoy some time in Vegas without having to be part of any crazy sect conflict, a pack of Sabbat Cainites with an awful lot of money stops in at the Venetian. As the characters venture out into the city, however, they find themselves harried and outnumbered by unfriendly Camarilla Kindred. They must return to the Venetian where it's ostensibly safe and try to enlist Dante's help getting safely back out of the city.

• A rumor begins to circulate in Las Vegas that Dante Giovanni has convinced an old and powerful Cathayan to visit the Venetian from his "new home" in San Francisco under the terms of a temporary truce. Local Cainite contacts believe that this mysterious Cathayan has come to discuss alliance or some other end to the conflicts brewing between Eastern and Western Kindred in California. Dubious of all of these claims, a mentor or authority figure over the players' characters' coterie asks the coterie to go to the Venetian and investigate. When they arrive, the characters are given reason to suspect that the rumors about a Cathayan guest were lies, and they must decide whether to expose Dante's scam or blackmail him with what they've discovered.

• Assuming that the setup is the same but that Dante Giovanni actually *has* convinced a Cathayan diplomat to visit the Venetian, the players' characters discover as much and make contact. They may discover that the Cathayan has come to the Venetian only as part of an attempted coup or that he's fleeing vengeful elders of his kind, whom he'd betrayed in California. The coterie can aid him in either endeavor, earning his grudging trust (and potentially an exotic new member of their coterie), or it can see that he fails in hopes of scoring points with the people who oppose him. Alternatively, the characters might learn that their rival sect plans to assassinate the diplomat and pin it on the coterie's sect in order to force that sect into a two-front conflict for territory. Finally, the characters themselves might be the agents provocateurs who have been ordered to commit murder by the elders of their own sect.

The Gatekeeper's Hold

Most Nosferatu in any given city choose to live in quiet, secluded areas or deep underground away from prying, scornful eyes. Occasionally, though, a Kindred of that clan cannot (or will not) live in the great Warrens with her brethren. Maximilian Spanner of Clan Nosferatu is just such a Kindred. Yet, even though he does not mingle with his clanmates in their dens, he is still a valuable asset to the clan.

Resident

Maximilian is moderately claustrophobic, which is an unenviable phobia for a Nosferatu, regardless of its severity. Because of his fear of enclosed spaces, Maximilian prefers to avoid the sewers and the Warrens as much as possible, and he absolutely refuses to live in the oppressive underground chambers that his peers normally frequent. Instead of striking out entirely on his own, though, Maximilian has established a haven close to the Warrens of his city with enough open room inside for him to avoid the pressures of his phobia. Many years ago Maximilian set up his haven in a water treatment plant.

The deformities that strike Clan Nosferatu have ravaged Maximilian. His face and body are strikingly changed from the human norm, leaving him little hope of engaging in normal interaction with the rest of humanity unless he is heavily disguised. Maximilian's skin droops from his bones, making it look ready to slough off entirely without warning. The effect is worst on his face, giving him a horribly weathered and scarred visage too gruesome to be mistaken for one ravaged by extreme old age. The loose skin around his mouth flaps when he moves his jaw, muffling his words and making feeding a difficult affair.

The deformities are so intense that most kine who have dealt face-to-face with Maximilian can hardly make out a word he's saying, even when he uses Obfuscate to spare them the horror of what he looks like. Since Maximilian's haven is a functioning water treatment plant, he must rely on Obfuscate quite often in order to deal with the average humans who make their living at the plant. In particular, Mask of a Thousand Faces serves Maximilian well, since he works as a night manager of the plant and is forced to deal with the kine on a regular basis.

Maximilian chose the water treatment plant for a number of reasons, not the least of which is the fact that he worked there at the time of his Embrace, and he has forced his way to a management position since that fateful night. By staying with the water treatment plant, he can dwell relatively close to his clan, yet far enough away to avoid actually living in the confines of the sewers. His claustrophobia is not so severe that he can't enter the sewers, but he is constantly on edge while there, always aware of each and every trickle or groan that the superstructure emits. Maximilian is all too aware of the other clans' antipathy toward the Nosferatu, and he wishes to stay as far away from Kindred society as his brethren do. Still, despite these misgivings, the insular nature of his clan dictates that he stay close to his blood brethren.

Another advantage of the water treatment plant is its relationship to the city's sewer system. The water treatment plant services over half a million people in the city by taking waste water, purifying it, adding chemicals, and preparing that water for use once again (even though it is not usually considered drinking water). The plant is connected to and monitors most of the city sewers, which places Maximilian in a position to help ensure the survival and well being of the local Nosferatu who dwell therein. He has a decent working relationship with just about every human he comes into regular contact with, especially the other plant managers and supervisors. The people at the water treatment plant are a gruff sort, and Maximilian's modicum of tact and charisma has won him a number of friends and loyal subordinates in his role as night-shift manager, even though he hardly ever speaks. With his influence in the plant, Maximilian can shut off or reroute any number of active sewers, making them safe for use by his clan.

A final advantage of the water treatment plant is that most of the people living in and around the city shun it. The wastewater that flows into the plant smells atrocious, and most people go out of their way to avoid it. Only cheap tract housing is built near the plant, and those houses are hard to sell despite their low prices. By and large, people don't care what goes on at the plant as long as their water is clean, their toilets flush, and their sewers carry all their detritus away.

Appearance

The plant itself is not a single building, but a series of buildings interconnected by a similar infrastructure. The buildings are composed almost entirely of aluminum, steel and concrete, making the plant very sturdy and not unlike a fortress. Yet, even though its defensibility is one of the most appealing aspects of the plant, there have been no incidents to date serious enough to constitute a need for such defense. Mostly, the sturdy architecture of the plant appeals to Maximilian's innate desire for security.

The plant's four different buildings are built on eight acres of land. In addition, a number of holding tanks stand beside the buildings in which the work of the plant is conducted. The tanks hold amounts of water ranging from hundreds to multiple thousands of gallons. Most of the larger tanks have open tops, and it is from these massive tanks that the telltale stench of the plant originates. Once wastewater from the sewers is pumped into the plant, it goes through a specific series of tanks that first filter, then purify, then chemically treat the water. That water is then re-released into the city's water system or into a nearby lake that serves as an even larger holding tank for the metropolitan area.

The largest and most important building in the complex is the Primary, a block of concrete and glass that's physically unremarkable except for its size. The Primary is where most of the work is performed and, consequently, where most of the workers can be found both day and night. The only entrances into the plant are through the Primary.

Layout

A small waiting room just inside the doors is where visitors and arriving workers are received and approved to pass through the heavy steel inner doors of the Primary building. Workers are issued an ID card with a magnetic strip on the back, and the card offers access to all the buildings and many of the service areas. Without a card, a visitor can get out of a building but not back into one.

Besides the one receiving entrance, a series of garages within the Primary can also be opened with the swipe of an ID card. Three large garages service the small fleet of trucks and carts that the workers use to move about the plant as well as to answer calls in and around the city. Keys to the trucks are under the care of the plant managers, one of whom, of course, is Maximilian. In his position at the plant, he is more than able to fill out (or forge) the necessary documents for requisitioning one or more of these trucks should the need arise.

Aside from the garage doors and the usual entrance (at which the shift guard can normally be found), the only way into the plant is through the sewer systems, most of which are in use at any given time. After dark, Maximilian makes sure that one sewer pipe is always open to allow the Nosferatu into the plant. If he needs to, Maximilian can have the plant crew flood that open pipe within minutes in order to close off this entrance. The pipe is exceptionally small, so Maximilian would rather die than crawl through its horribly cramped confines. Instead, whenever he must go into the sewers, he uses other entrances outside the complex.

Most of the work at the plant occurs on the first level of the Primary. Water-system monitoring is conducted using large maps of the plant and the city sewer system. Multiple just-out-of-date computers aid the workers in the routine maintenance and review of the plant. Also within the Primary are the garages and a large storeroom where most of the heavier equipment is kept. Occasionally, city engineers not associated with the water treatment plant pose a problem as they perform their jobs in and around the Primary. Maximilian usually informs the city's Nosferatu of the situation and allows more politically connected clanmates to subtly avert any potential trouble.

More piping and tubes than one can count run through the first basement level of the Primary so that the workers can have easy access to the most critical systems and junctions. Along with the many pipes, a couple of circuit breakers and the telephone frame are also on this level. Otherwise, the only aspects of the basement worth noting are the large, locked steel doors that lead to Maximilian's haven, which is disguised as a mechanical closet. Although the doors look old and rusted, they are in quite good repair and very sturdy where it counts. To break down the reinforced doors requires a Strength roll against a difficulty of 10, and the character attempting to break down the door must have at least one dot in Potence. Picking the door locks is much easier, as it requires only a Dexterity + Security roll (difficulty 7).

Each evening as the shifts change, Maximilian uses Obfuscate to leave the Primary. Outside, he finds an out-of-sight alcove, uses Mask of a Thousand Faces to create his "normal" visage and reenters the plant through the entrance. He checks in, waves hello to the people who are already at work and then gets to work himself. By two or three hours into his shift, Maximilian has taken care of his nightly paperwork and can oversee the plant at his leisure. After midnight, he often discreetly disappears for some time to take care of any Kindred matters with which his clanmates might have chosen to burden him. Only a handful of people who work at the plant know Maximilian personally. Most know him by his positive reputation. Those who do know him personally are on good terms with him, seeing him as friendly, competent and a remarkably good listener.

Maximilian's Haven

Maximilian sleeps and spends most of his time in one of the larger rooms in the deepest basement, to which only the managers have access, and which supposedly serves as an unused and out-of-the-way mechanical closet. Of the plant's managers, only Maximilian has keys to this particular room. Its location, coupled with the fact that the truly useful equipment other employees might need is stored elsewhere, all but ensures that the plant workers stay away. Despite his mild phobia of tight spaces, Maximilian's need to establish a haven safely away from the sun and not in danger of discovery necessitated his use of the lowermost basement. And necessity, in this case, outweighs convenience.

The haven itself is one large room about the size of a two-bedroom apartment, with a 12-foot-tall ceiling. The lack of dividing walls and the high ceiling help alleviate Maximilian's phobia, but the fact that he is cooped up underground still gets to him every evening when he wakes.

In the haven, Maximilian keeps a good-sized cot to sleep on, but he doesn't bother with a blanket or pillows, because he doesn't wake up any more or less comfortable than he was when he went to sleep. The day manager, Tony Athlex, knows that Maximilian often sleeps in the mechanical closet, but he was convinced some time ago to look the other way. Tony believes that Maximilian is having some personal trouble at home and that ignoring the existence of the cot is a huge favor he's doing his coworker. Maximilian's ability to persuade Tony so easily springs not only from a well-conceived story, but also from the partial blood bond that Max enforces by mixing his vitae with the coffee he hands to Tony as they switch shifts.

Besides the cot in the center of the room, a number of modern computers line the walls. With these, Maximilian monitors all the happenings of the plant and can access the series of cameras that watch key spots within the compound. In his role as night-shift manager, Max spends much of his time helping to program and tinker with the security cameras, so it was easy for him to set up a patch to the computers in his haven.

What other furniture Maximilian has in the haven has all been pushed against the walls, helping to maintain the room's open feel. It includes a worn set of bookshelves, a dilapidated couch, a small end table acting as a nightstand, and a tall, wide mirror that Maximilian scrounged from a nearby tract house that burned down and had to be refurbished. The mirror gives the illusion of enlarging the room further. The only furniture in the middle of the floor is the cot. He keeps it there because if he pushed it against a wall or into a corner, the sensation of waking up with walls looming over him would trigger a panic attack.

The air-recycling system broke down a number of years ago, and since Maximilian has no need to breathe, has not seen fit to fix it. Consequently, the air in the sub-basement is stale and thin, as it's only refreshed whenever someone opens the steel doors to the upper basement. In some respects, the atmosphere resembles that of a tomb. The air within remains relatively cool because the room is so far underground, though Maximilian is occasionally forced to keep the doors open for nights on end during the summer to help cool the computers. At these times, he is most on edge. He has started to consider using a more advanced water cooling system to help alleviate any overheating problems, but for the time being, the intrusion on his personal space and the money involved to build such a system is prohibitive.

The Gatehouse

More than just a place to stay, Maximilian's haven serves a greater purpose for the Nosferatu of the city. Maximilian chose the water treatment plant for a number of reasons, security being paramount. Yet, beyond his own physical security, the plant can also regulate much of the city's water infrastructure. This ability to monitor and affect the flow of water through the many sewers has served the Nosferatu well and accorded Maximilian a good deal of status within the clan. By virtue of his haven's utility, Maximilian is a valued Nosferatu, and his eccentric desire to live outside the sewers is tolerated because of the service he provides.

Furthermore, Maximilian is on good terms with nearly all the Nosferatu architects, the ones who modify and expand upon the Warrens that lace the city. Their visions of underground labyrinths are made a reality with the help of Maximilian and the water treatment plant. At the planning stages for expansion of the Warrens, a number of sewer lines are identified as needing to be blocked off to create a dry environment. Instead of having to physically block the pipes, as many Nosferatu in other cities must do, the architects simply contact Maximilian and tell him what they need. If he can arrange it, he then reroutes the water from those pipes.

Not only is this method more efficient for the Nosferatu, but it also helps divert any kine attention that unexpected interruption of water services may bring. By working through the water treatment plant, Maximilian can reroute water safely with little interruption of water services to the seething masses above. Through the other plant managers, Maximilian also has the ability to request that work crews avoid certain "sensitive" areas of the sewers, making sure that little chance exists of some unwitting sewer work team uncovering the Warrens. Because of his actions, humans remain ignorant of the continued building that goes on under their city.

Feeding

The major disadvantage of the water treatment plant is the static environment it creates, which makes it difficult for Maximilian to gather a large herd to secure his feeding needs. Aside from the five plant managers (who have all been mildly blood-bound), there are few kine upon whom he can rely to provide sustenance. Like most Kindred, Maximilian's primary concern is to feed in relative security and minimize the chance of inadvertent discovery. Maximilian is savvy enough to know not to feed from his co-workers except in the direst emergencies.

Therefore, Maximilian feeds almost exclusively off the people in the tract housing near the plant. He looks forward to the evenings when he can come up with an appropriate excuse to leave the plant, because then he can walk outside his protective walls and alleviate his claustrophobia entirely for a while. Usually, he just uses Obfuscate and strolls into the tract housing, but on rare occasions he drives one of the plant's many pickup trucks. Even then, he's careful to park the truck somewhere dark and secluded from the houses within which he intends to dine. If he happens to kill his victim, it wouldn't do to have such an easily traceable piece of evidence nearby where witnesses might happen upon it.

Security

Much of the plant's security is passive. A large, chain-link fence eight feet high rings the entire plant. Razorwire lines the top of the fence in lazy coils, an obvious attempt to keep the idle curious out, though the stench of the wastewater performs this function better than any fence. The razorwire is not a new feature, but this particular length of it was recently replaced in reaction to the September 11th attacks in New York. A more mundane and realistic concern is the recurrent petty crime and domestic disturbances in the low-cost housing around the plant. The city's municipal committee sees fences, wire and other security measures as a necessary expense to safeguard the computer equipment used to regulate the sewers and treatment process. Between occasional criminal acts and the policymakers' (over-inflated) fear of terrorism, the city has also hired two paid guards to watch over the plant, one for the day and one for the night shifts. Maximilian has established a good relationship with the night-shift guard, and he welcomes the additional security.

More important than the security measures protecting the plant are the security provided by the water treatment plant to the Nosferatu Warrens to which it's connected. After all, a number of the major entrances into the Warrens begin in or around the water treatment plant. Maximilian is more than happy to monitor these entrances for his own security as well as for the Warrens. While Maximilian has little power to stop a determined interloper, he can contact the Warrens through a secure phone line in his haven and call for help. Should anything out of the ordinary arise, the night watchman and the plant workers know to report directly to Max. With this extra help and his cameras, Maximilian has a good idea of all goings-on in and around the major entrances to the Warrens.

Should the Warrens actually be besieged, Maximilian is prepared to come to the aid of the Warrens in his own way. Even though he is not physically strong, Maximilian can still aid his Nosferatu brethren from inside the confines of the water treatment plant. By flooding certain key pipelines, Maximilian can cut off any major routes of attack, slowing an invasion considerably. Additionally, the water treatment plant can be used for a counteroffensive. Maximilian can flood the pipes that the invaders are using. If they breathe air, they are highly likely to drown. If they do not breathe, the swift flow of the water may be enough to sweep them off their feet and deposit them outside the sewers, or at least into a waiting ambush of angry Nosferatu.

Story Ideas

• In preparation for an invasion of the city, leaders in the Sabbat hope to seize dominance of the invaluable sewer ways leading back and forth beneath it. To test the waters, so to speak, a pack of Cainites is sent into the sewers through the water treatment plant on a reconnaissance mission. They make it through the plant and into the sewers easily enough, but once there, they find the place practically coming to life and turning against them. Realizing they've been set up by someone at the plant and that they'd have to be crazy to forge ahead, the members of the pack must defy expectations and head back out toward the water treatment plant. If they can deal with whoever is waiting at the plant, they might just ease their compatriots' seizure of the rest of the sewers.

- Over several weeks, Maximilian's contact with residents of the Warrens dwindles until it finally cuts off altogether. He waits for another week in growing alarm until finally a young, terrified Nosferatu stumbles into the plant, wild-eyed and ranting about an enormous, silent… *something* preying on the Kindred of the Warrens. Unwilling to enter the sewers himself (especially if something dangerous is prowling around down there), Max is quick to call upon a brave and able coterie to investigate for him and tell him what's going on.

- In a move designed to put pressure on the local Nosferatu and figuratively force them to the surface of Kindred society (rather than skulking together underground planning God-knows-what), the local prince installs a blood-bound ghoul as the head of the water treatment plant. This ghoul has the power to fire Maximilian, and he keeps an eye out to curtail Maximilian's ability to screw around with the city's water. Rather than bow and scrape to the prince's subsequent inquiries and demands, however, the Nosferatu are riled, and they take a more guerrilla-warfare approach. Their first tactic is to have Maximilian imprison the prince's ghoul and shut off water to certain parts of the city. Their next step, they warn, will be to start tampering with the filters that clean the city's water unless the prince leaves them alone. In response, the prince assembles a coterie of level-headed young vampires to go to the water treatment plant and try to reason with the Nosferatu on his behalf through Maximilian.

The House that Fear Built

Once upon a time, two mortal brothers lived together in a dilapidated house. One was an invalid who relied on his sibling for all the basic needs in life. The other was insane, and he filled their home with a cluttered maze of papers, magazines and furniture. Afraid of theft, the ambulatory brother booby-trapped his collection, turning stacks of paper and wood into a potential avalanche to bury unsuspecting thieves. The traps backfired, however, when the physically capable brother tripped one pitfall and lay pinned beneath a ton of paper. He died because his invalid brother could not save him, while the bed-ridden sibling in turn died from starvation in a pool of his own filth.

Amateurs…

Resident

Every city has a neighborhood whose sole purpose is to embody the lost glory of yesteryear. Once, baroque and art deco mansions lined their avenues. Manicured trees provided shade to local children, and chic women walked the streets while showing off their new button-up, knee-high leg gaiters, Palm Beach fashions with low hemlines or recently purchased Dolcis shoes. Unfortunately, memories of these lost golden years died away in the Depression or became casualties of the no-nonsense sensibilities of the 1950s. Slumlords turned the once luxurious mansions into smaller apartments for the milling throngs of the impoverished who flocked into these decaying bastions of white-collar life like rats to land from a sinking ship. Eventually, the only testimony to these neighborhoods' former greatness remained in the faded black-and-white snapshots of times gone by, the little frieze trim still adorning some apartments or the filth-covered building facades that only occasionally betrayed some hint of their past glory.

Harriet Perkins once lived in the largest home of one such suburb, but her Embrace and subsequent descent into Malkavian insanity mirrored the neighborhood's decline during the Great Depression. Blessed with old money, her blue-blooded family, which was now ghouled to her whims, purchased every available mansion that came up for sale, until she owned everything within the cluster of blocks that surrounded her own. The Perkins family then converted all the mansions, save theirs, of course, into smaller apartments in order to support the ghetto that was blossoming around them. Every home they converted devalued the local property further, making it easier to purchase more buildings. For Harriet, the role of slumlord proved profitable both financially and in terms of vitae. Her tenants, mostly North American untouchables, were no more important than cobwebs. When they vanished, few bothered to investigate or even cared.

Over the years, Harriet has existed in her mansion, growing more reclusive with each decade. She still owns buildings throughout the neighborhoods, and sells them off one at a time when finances require. Others she has lost to drug dealers or to the courts when a group of tenants has the courage to rail against their squalid living conditions. Some buildings are outright condemned from the near-century of neglect. Still, Harriet's current properties are enough to sustain her and the few family members still around. Thanks to the timely payment of well-placed bribes and the efforts of a few ghoul proxies who act as intermediaries, her building enjoys relative freedom from city inspectors or the police.

Appearance

From the street, Harriet's five-story apartment mansion looks no different than the other buildings that line the block. A witness trained in architecture, however, should notice that many of its art nouveau influences still remain despite the decades of neglect that the place has weathered. Inspired by natural and seamless architecture, the building façade bears few angled lines. Instead, ledges merge into outcroppings such as the projecting rectangular bay windows, while the windows themselves are all vertical and thin with soft corners. A wide-ledge cornice runs along the lip of the roof, but the classic floral-pattern frieze that the original craftsmen sculpted into the stone has long since been worn away by pollution and age. A cake of filth and soot hides what could undoubtedly become a historic site if anyone were to take the time to renovate it. Few outsiders venture down to this crime-ridden district willingly, though, so nobody really notices or seems to care.

The natural fluidity of the art nouveau style lends the building a slightly organic look, but the bricked-up windows and the wrought-iron gates that cover the door make its foreboding quality even more acute. The gates are also of a style with the structure, their whiplash vine curves and flowery blooms blackened by age. Additionally, Harriet's family cut jagged patterns into the vines and frames, sharpened the edges, and soldered the screws so that nobody could simply unfasten the gates. Consequently, anyone who did try to remove the gates with a level-four feat of Strength would have to rip them off, which in turn would shred their hands to bloody strips on the jagged edges (which translates to taking three dice of bashing damage).

In addition to being bricked up, the windows are blocked by heavy furniture and years worth of junk. The only ways to get inside are by walking through the front door or climbing in through the single oculus (circular window) at the top front of the building.

Layout

While the building exterior is definitively art nouveau in style, the interior relies on more traditional designs. Unfortunately, any trimmings that might once have adorned the interior are now either gone or hidden beneath the cluttered filth. Yet, Harriet is more than just a packrat. She is cursed with Malkavian-borne delusions, and she fully believes that she leaves behind portions of her soul on whatever she touches (including furniture, paper, bits of trash, knickknacks and even family members). To protect herself, she collects, buys, steals or kidnaps anything she enjoys or might happen to touch, thus keeping her "soul" from scattering into a thousand tiny fragments.

Over the years, this fear has grown considerably, and Harriet has secluded herself in her home in order to preserve the lingering remnants of her being. Her mansion is a terrible, squalid and decaying pile of almost everything she's collected over the decades. Moreover, she protects her property from theft by booby-trapping everything. Her ghouls might die as a result of occasional missteps, but she is willing to endure this nuisance, if only because their bodies belong to her anyway. That is, they too possess portions of Harriet through their service to her. Eventually, Harriet's delusions will reach a point at which she simply kills or kidnaps anyone who comes into contact with her, treating them like stockpiled property.

Of the mansion itself, little beauty remains. The gilt walls and floral wallpaper have long since faded into streaked and water-stained obscurity or been chipped away under a hundred minute stresses, while the wood-covered floors and ceilings have lost their shiny veneer and are now warped or gap-toothed. Most of the interior lights have burned out, and even if one of her ghouls were inclined to change some of them, they are no longer within reach thanks to the piles of refuse. Rats are constantly underfoot, while pigeons have sneaked in through one window. Harriet does not mind these vermin, however, since they serve as quick snacks or capable ghouls if no one else comes immediately to hand.

The Main Floor

The only available entrance to the mansion on the main floor is the front door, which requires a Dexterity + Security roll (difficulty 5) to break into. A character could also use the back door or one of the windows, but he would need to put an hour or two into clearing the piles of detritus out of the way. The blockaded windows and few operating lights cast the mansion into darkness and ubiquitous shadows. Harriet can see easily in the unlit interior, and she can navigate the cramped corridors with her eyes shut. She is intimately familiar with her environment, after all, as well as possessing an almost eidetic memory of her collection and the location of specific items.

Visitors, including Harriet's ghouls, must use flashlights to circumnavigate the maze, and even then, the ghouls know specifically which paths are safe from booby traps. Naturally, the maze begins upon entry to the building.

The Foyer

The foyer is typically large enough for three or four people to stand in comfortably, and it is one of the few spots on the first floor that is relatively open. A rosewood coat-and-hat rack of American Victorian Revival design (1840 to 1880) stands there, its wood dry and cracked. Moth-eaten coats and hats still rest on the rack, in memoriam to former visitors who never left this place. Searching through the pockets of these coats might reveal a matchbox from a club that closed or a receipt from a restaurant that went out of business some 20 or 30 years ago.

The antique pedigree of the rack hints at the Perkins' wealth. Had Harriet tended to them properly, this and other objects would have fetched a high price in specialty stores and possibly even museums. The Perkins family had class and fine tastes, and the mansion is now a treasure trove of antiques. Most belonged to the Perkinses, themselves, while they purchased other items at cutthroat rates from rich families whose fortunes faltered during the Depression. Harriet, however, will savage and kill anyone who tries to steal "a portion of her soul," and she has done so before. She does not care about its condition, as long as the item in question remains in her care.

The Reception Hall

Once, when the mansion was new and in good repair, the foyer opened into a large and airy hall that was three stories high. An open archway to the left led into the sitting room for guests, while a set of wide Imperial stairs opposite the foyer split off at the landing and spiraled upward as two smaller staircases to the fourth story. Doors on either side of the stairwell led away to the servants' quarters and the kitchen. To the right, another archway revealed a sumptuous dining hall. On either side of the foyer rested rectangular bay window alcoves with sofas for more intimate conversations. The gilt walls, floral friezes, four spiral columns and slightly arched ceiling with its angelic-motif fresco brightened and enlivened the interior and put guests at ease.

Unfortunately, however, age, darkness and clutter now hide the overall effect, leaving visitors to discover these various elements only after stumbling upon them by accident. A maze of random turns and curving side-passages cuts haphazardly through the disarray. Most of these paths are wide enough for only one person to walk through at a time, while others force people to move sideways through them. The maze consists of reams of stacked newspapers and magazines, boxes filled with knickknacks, loose silverware, clothing and balanced furniture that ranges from chairs to bookshelves and even to several grand pianos. This motley assortment of items forms precarious walls that reach irregular heights of two to three meters.

Climbing these obstacles is not an option. Harriet's ghouls have recently laced many of the walls with rows of barbed wire, and those walls will collapse and take out a large area in true domino form if someone places too much weight on them. While this style of simple booby trap may not seem threatening to creatures such as vampires, the combination of heavy furniture and sharp corners is enough to dish out big punishment (not to mention the pain of entangling oneself in barbed wire). A falling wall inflicts eight dice of bashing damage. Additionally, there is only one safe way through the corridors, and many of the twisting passages have been strung with trip wires that are carefully rigged to bring the clutter crashing down. Spotting and avoiding these trip wires requires a Perception + Alertness roll (difficulty 9).

The ceiling fresco is faded in many places, or worn straight through to the floorboards of the story above. Harriet often spies on visitors or thieves through the larger holes, and she possesses an excellent vantage from this position.

The stairway, with its metal, flowery balustrade and two unlit lamps on thick posts, is also covered with boxes and piles of paper. It looks like the scene of a garbage-dump landslide. Making one's way upstairs, which the ghouls avoid doing altogether since the upstairs is Harriet's domain, is a feat of acrobatics across the few clear spots.

Sitting Room and Dining Room

These two large rooms once existed solely for the entertainment of guests, while the Perkins' family life centered around the third floor. The Perkinses used the sitting room for occasional dances, which Harriet remembers fondly and sometimes forces the few surviving family ghouls to reenact with her. Now, though, these chambers are little more than extensions of the main hall. The maze of detritus runs throughout these areas as well, though the sitting room does have a small oasis of relatively uncluttered space.

The bare spot in question is in the room's center, where Harriet keeps a 10-square-foot space clear. Here, the marble floor has an inlaid golden sunburst pattern that once served as the dazzling highlight of the chamber. To one side of the space rests an old record player with a sparse collection of dusty vinyl albums dating back to the '20s and '30s. Many of the records are now broken or badly scratched, but that doesn't stop Harriet from dancing to the skipping, hiccuping beats. Her music collection showcases diverse talents from the brass and horns of Percival Mackey's Band and the Five Aces, to orchestral composers such as Beethoven and Prokofiev.

These two rooms hold a wealth of battered and worn antiques. Some of the highlights include a Victorian parlor cabinet with a cracked cameo adorning the front, a complete living room set of Federal-style mahogany furniture dating back to 1809, a Hepplewhite cabinet from the late 1700s and silverware (as well as bronze and pewter-ware) from Tiffany & Company and the International Silver Company. While this variety and distinction may mean nothing to common thieves or children of the modern nights, shrewd vampires can curry favors from elders by offering as gifts reworked antiques salvaged from the Perkins estate. The nostalgia factor alone for these items is enormous, not to mention their potential worth in any market. Even someone trying to sell something as innocuous as a stolen Steiff teddy bear or Amelung engraved tumbler might find himself under scrutiny from collectors who understand these items' true value. Frankly, it is a wonder that Harriet has managed to keep her treasure trove of antiques a secret thus far, given that a few wily thieves have actually escaped her haven unnoticed. A few of the same are even bold enough to return on occasion, stealing and fencing knickknacks to provide them with a quick grand now and again.

The Servants' Quarters

A small and relatively uncluttered — yet still squalid — hallway connects to three small bedrooms, a communal living room, a shared bathroom and an exit that leads into a back alley. A neo-classic high chest filled with old books currently barricades the door, but Harriet's ghouls can open this exit easily by removing the filled drawers and pushing the cabinet to the side. This area once served as servants' quarters for the head maid, the house cook and the nanny, but now it is a squatter's den for any homeless mortals that the ghouls can manage to lure here on occasion. While the soiled mattresses, broken plumbing and unheated rooms would frighten most sensible folk away, the ghouls prey on the crack-heads or runaways who don't know any better. The lucky guests rarely last the night, while the unfortunate ones must play a dangerous game of cat and mouse with Harriet in the maze of junk. To date, no human has survived that deadly ordeal.

The Kitchen

Understandably, Harriet's ghouls prefer to live elsewhere, even if they must live in the slums that surround the mansion. At least those accommodations beat this rat- and pigeon-infested warren (if only barely). When the ghouls left, the kitchen simply became another storage space for silverware and boxed items. Of course, clutter blocks the kitchen's alley exit, but the ghouls hammered nails into the door and frame years ago for added security.

Anyone unfamiliar with Harriet's peculiarities might be surprised to hear fluttering and other sounds of movement coming from the large refrigerator (now left unplugged), or from the pantry. If a guest opens either, a grisly sight awaits in the form of half-dead, half-eaten and decomposing pigeons, rats and the occasional cat, all of which has been strewn across the ample shelves or floor. Harriet catches critters in her spare time, either ghouling some when she can spare the blood or storing them in the refrigerator and meat locker for later consumption. The panicked animals feed off each other or perish when Harriet drains them and tosses their carcasses back inside.

Second Floor

Where the first floor is a maze, the second floor (fourth story) is more or less an abattoir. As her mortal family members passed away, Harriet laid them to rest in their rooms and simply closed their doors. Even now, she visits them nightly (if only to chase away or sup on the rats within). She even goes to the trouble of changing their clothing every few months.

The second floor was the family residence where Harriet, her parents and three siblings lived. Following her Embrace, however, Harriet convinced immediate (and then extended) family members to live in the mansion like one giant, happy, cramped community. Harriet's influence turned them into degenerate ghouls, and few managed to escape her maddening touch. Those who are still around survived only by moving out of the mansion. They convinced Harriet that their skills better served her outside, although their blood conditioning and her influence over them brings them inexorably back every few days to feed her. When they are too drained of vitae, the ghouls bring in a squatter or two to sustain Harriet instead.

The mansion's grandeur is far more evident on this floor, with faded maple and oak paneling, arched ceilings and worn Kirman Persian carpets covering the hardwood floor. A layer of crusted dust coats the gilt walls, some with art deco flair in the silver chevron sunrise patterns that run the length of the hallways. Age still claims its share of the mansion's luster, of course, but the extent of its ravages here is a far cry from the dilapidation of the lower levels.

Bedrooms

The mansion holds five bedrooms and one master bedroom on the second floor, essentially three rooms per hallway (which run parallel to one another on either side of the stairs). In most rooms, half-columns of Doric design emerge from the walls on marble bases, while a cavernous fireplace graces the master bedroom. Except for one, the rooms are makeshift mausoleums that now house at least four dead family members per chamber. The bodies of the deceased rest on the four-poster beds, reposed beneath threadbare blankets, or slouched in worn French-Empire style armchairs. Harriet cleans the cobwebs out when she can, but she can never chase away the swarms of rats that remain hidden in the hollows of the walls. The rats' incessant squeaking echoes throughout the rooms, but Harriet has grown quite used to their "gay chatter."

The last room belongs to Harriet, and she has slept in it since the '20s. It is her haven proper. Devoid of windows and possessed of one working bulb hidden beneath a dust-shrouded shade, the room remains in an eerie twilight of weak light and deep shadows. Her favorite toys, from cracked porcelain dolls to bears that are bleeding stuffing, adorn the shelves and chairs where they share space with rats and an empty pigeon's nest. The large dining table's stained doily covers the four-poster bed like makeshift mosquito netting, while a wind-up gramophone rests on the nightstand.

Even in the near-perfect darkness that obscures it, Harriet knows where to walk safely inside the room. Visitors, however, must be careful not to trip on a couple of holes that lie hidden beneath the carpet. The carpet is easy to roll back, revealing missing floorboards and spy holes through the ceiling below (the fresco). If Harriet knows that someone is in the house, she watches the intruder from this point, marking his passage. Whenever she's downstairs, she glances casually up at her spy holes every few minutes, as if she's lost herself in thought.

Study

Before his death, Mister Perkins ran the family business from his study. His old Davenport mahogany desk is impressive despite the clutter of yellowed papers that litter its surface. Brittle, crumbling files fill the drawers, although they contain little of importance save the odd deed to a local building. Unfortunately, nearby gangs and crack-dealers have more of a hold on neighborhood buildings than Harriet does, so claiming any property would be difficult at best for her.

Aside from Mister Perkins' desk, a giant mounted wooden globe and a reading sofa occupy the room. The study's four walls also hold shelves filled with books. Their condition varies from fair to poor, but the books are first editions, or they possess dust jackets before standardization in 1910, or they are leather-bound hardbacks, or they are adorned with fake but elaborate jewel-work on the spine and cover. Again, this collection could be worth a fortune to the greedy, but the sudden appearance of these rare items on the market will attract undue attention from curious collectors.

The Family Room

This room was the center of Harriet's life as a child, for it was here that her family gathered in the evenings. The original décor remains, with Neo-Grecian seats and sofas bearing distinctive wide-ledge seating and curled-lip armrests. Harriet's fondest memories revolve around this room, which she keeps cluttered with such nostalgic items as scattered albums and boxes of photos, a 1936 Sparton 527-2 radio (black, art-deco style, it looks a little like an old radiator) and a 1906 Chickering Parlor Grand pianoforte. Harriet, an accomplished pianist, still practices and often plays for her ghouls, although it's up to them to keep the instrument in tune.

The Attic

Hidden down a short hallway is a locked door that leads into the attic. Harriet has the key, but anyone with enough determination (and a strong shoulder, of course) can easily break through the door to reach the set of rickety wooden stairs beyond. A horrific smell pervades the hallway, the odors of fecal matter and decay.

The open attic is part storage space and part charnel house for Harriet's victims. She dumps their bodies here once she's finished with them, then allows the rats, pigeons and roaches to feed on the decaying mass. At least two dozen bodies are scattered around the attic, all in various states of decomposition. Should someone with a good eye for detail investigate, he would be able to tell that the bodies range in post-mortem age from 70 years to less than a month.

Harriet also stores boxes and newspapers in the attic, but she keeps all of those precious items covered in tarps and plastic sheets. The fact that she does so is good, because the rats and pigeons that line the wooden beams have layered everything in a coat of waste matter. During the summer, the ghouls constantly scatter baking soda to dampen the smell — otherwise, the stench would definitely attract attention. During winter, the cold is enough to hem in the local rodent population and kill the odors as well.

The attic boasts the only window through which one might gain unimpeded entry into the house, but reaching it entails climbing up the support columns to the wooden beams, which are covered in pigeon and rat feces. Doing so during the day is almost a plea to get caught. Sneaking in this way might be easier at night, but the intruder would then have to skulk through the house in full dark while Harriet is likely watching.

Won't You Come In?

Bearing in mind Harriet's eccentricities and her "devotion" to her home, it is hard to believe that Cainites would have any occasion to visit. Such is not the case, however. Harriet is the daughter of a local Malkavian of some repute, so she enjoys his protection. Furthermore, Harriet has not been active in local Kindred society for so long that few long-time residents likely remember her.

Having realized that isolation is a terrible burden to endure, Harriet's sire has decided that Harriet needs new acquaintances to help keep her occupied. To that end, he approaches fledgling Malkavians or other neonates, asking them to "keep an old woman company in her lonely hours." He considers acquiescence to this request a personal favor, although he has been known to seek out young Kindred who disparage his clan and put them on the spot with his request in front of their respected elders.

While Harriet may not appreciate visitors, she knows better than to argue with her sire, who has offered her considerable leeway in regards to her feeding habits over the past decades. She agrees to entertain the visitors on the single condition that they follow her rules (a fact that her sire stresses to the neonates). Harriet has her visitors blindfolded, then escorts them through the maze, giving them precise instructions on how many steps to take in which direction, as well as when to duck or where to put their hands for balance. In this way, she leads them upstairs to the family room. If the neonates behave and treat her with respect, she shows them photo albums (many of which are not her own), plays the piano and asks them to help her change her family's clothing. Eventually she even invites them to dance with her downstairs in an eerie sort of pantomime in which she does her best not to touch her newfound partner. If any of her guests are hungry… well, there's always food in the refrigerator.

Story Ideas

• A surly Kindred who was pressured into a harrowing visit with Harriet tells a group of his associates from out of town (i.e., the players' characters) about the wealth of antiques and vintage knickknacks that are just lying around the place begging to be stolen. He offers to set the characters up with a respectable fence and to give them the details of the house's layout if they'll break into the mansion, grab some of the items he suggests and cut him in on the profits of the heist.

• A dealer in antiques and rare books, who also happens to be a contact of Harriet's sire, alerts him that an unusually large number of rare first-edition books have been coming his way for certification of authenticity lately from the same shady collector. Harriet's sire recognizes many of the titles and editions from Harriet's collection, and he discovers later that those books have been stolen from her. Desperate to have the books found and returned before Harriet realizes that they're gone, he enlists the players' characters' coterie. He gives them a list of the Kindred he asked to spend time with Harriet lately as a roster of potential suspects and urges them to be as thorough, discreet and expeditious as possible in their investigation.

• While the characters are visiting Harriet at her sire's request, she informs them that her ghouls caught two little boys sneaking around downstairs that day while she slept. The ghouls had originally planned to keep the children around for Harriet's dinner that evening, but when they told her about it, she came up with a more "entertaining" idea. Knowing that she was expecting guests, she had her ghouls drug and hide the children somewhere in the house without telling her where. She plans to give her guests a one-hour head start and challenge them to find the children before she does — the winner gets to keep them to do with as he or she pleases. While she won't force her guests to play this game with her, characters with high Humanity ratings might feel compelled to take up the challenge just to get the children safely out of Harriet's clutches.

CVN 70, USS Carl Vinson

The United States Navy refers to its aircraft carriers as "floating cities," and this appellation holds true. With a crew of over 6,000 people and the capacity to service escort vessels, aircraft and naval movements, these behemoths of the ocean qualify not only as massive ships, but as catacomb-like villages that would rival a medieval town in size and population.

Among such quarters, a risky existence is possible for a vampire, though only the best concealment skills and the most careful planning allow a Cainite to evade detection among the cramped quarters and military precision. Influencing the staff isn't an option, since aberrant behavior among ship captains quickly draws notice and consequences.

Deep in the bowels of the ship, miles of piping and insulation worm through the engine room. Air-conditioning ducts, security passages and crawlspaces make a mazelike set of passages in and through multiple walls and decks. It's even possible to climb from tube to pipe high above the deck floors in the tall engineering compartments, walking or crawling in an occluded set of splitting, intersecting and merging cylinders broader than a man. A lone Assamite slinks through this labyrinthine property, proclaiming it the heart of his domain.

Resident

A 900-year-old Ottoman Turk makes his lair in the bowels of this floating fortress. Burak, a former Sufi Muslim and eccentric Assamite, chose this house of war as his den of peace.

Indoctrinated into the Assamite clan for his fierce devotion to his ideals and his dedicated asceticism (which gave him a powerfully strong will), Burak learned the Assamite way over the course of a century during the days when Constantinople changed hands. Much to the disappointment of his sire, however, he did not make a good killer. Too much of his religious training remained, and his conscience stayed his hand whenever he felt he could safely avoid conflict. After three-quarters of a century, he escaped from his disgusted sire and entered voluntary torpor. Convinced that his disappointing childe had perished while trying to escape, his sire moved on with his unlife.

Stuck in turgid, strange dreams, Burak remained in torpor for an unusually long time. As centuries passed, he slept in disused old Turkish crypts and didn't awaken until the late 1800s. Adjusting to the new industrial age took him the better part of the decade, and he was little more than a feral beast when he first rose. Only clinging to his principles allowed him to claw his way back to rationality. Although the world had changed, he still believed in his purpose, and he kept that purpose as his guiding center.

Fleeing Turkey by passenger liner, Burak became something of a nomadic sailor — working passage below decks here, booking a trip along the coastlines there. From time to time, he ran afoul of other Kindred, but as often as not, they gave him a wide berth because of his bloodline. They assumed he was the worst sort of bloodthirsty assassin on the prowl, and he rarely bothered to correct their mistaken impressions of him.

By the modern age, Burak had come to two conclusions. First, he realized that vampiric society was innately degrading and that it would serve only to erode the morals of anyone who participated in its Jyhad. Second, he saw in the onslaught of pollution, the threat of atomic warfare and the godlessness of the masses that the end of the world was at hand. Faced with those revelations, Burak decided to rely on his earliest lessons as an ascetic. If the world had become corrupt, he decided, then he must withdraw from the world.

After hiding among the outbuildings of a naval base, Burak finally decided to slip aboard the newly commissioned *Carl Vinson*. In this self-sufficient floating city he dreamed of isolating himself far away from any other Kindred. He would sail the oceans, remote from the decaying world, and he would practice a stern discipline and austerity, surrounded by mortals who practiced similar discipline.

Appearance

The sides of the *Carl Vinson* are gray metal walls, its deck painted with stripes and lined with running lights to guide aircraft. Its seven-story observation tower rises from the portside aft like the miniature airport control tower that it is. Along the fore, F-14D Tomcats and F/A-18 Hornets crowd about, prepared for strike roles, and E2C Hawkeye survey planes and HH-60H Seahawk helicopters stay clamped and ready to be called into action. The starboard side is a running airstrip with launch catapults and cabling. A fifth of a mile long, the ship looks like a jutting strip of metal road rising from a cable-strewn and slanted hull.

Inside, the halls are cramped and low. Sailors have to duck their heads as they walk, maintenance personnel constantly crowd the tiny corners and nooks, and rooms hold Spartan bunks. Even the meeting halls and mess rooms are compact. Ceilings rarely reach above six feet in height, and some hallways are even a few inches shorter. The doorways are oval hatches only four and a half feet high, and the crew quarters feature double bunks with footlockers and just enough room to stand. Everything's a military gray. Conservation of space is the order of the day. Common hallways and doors have rounded corners, but in other places, edges are still prominent and it's the sailor's job to pay attention when he's in a hurry, lest he win himself a trip to the infirmary. Ladders, not stairways, move from level to level.

The observation rooms of the tower and the command decks are boxes of close-packed electronics with crystalline plastic windows that overlook the deck and the sea. Facing the controls gives an observer the sense of claustrophobia present throughout the ship, while turning to face the windows lets one look out to the horizon. On these levels, the ship's operators and flag officers work, guiding the vessel, overseeing its pilots and electronics operators, and coordinating the ship's movements with fleet command.

Layout

Naval vessels must, by definition, economize. There's almost no spare room, and every inch is mapped somewhere on a blueprint. Fortunately for an enterprising Kindred, blueprints change, bulkheads are sealed off due to design changes and engine-room cabling is huge enough to make its own forest of metal and plastic.

On deck is about the worst place for any Kindred to be. It's open and unshielded, people are always out and about — generally, just over 100 flight and maintenance crew — and it basically has all the disadvantages of standing around at an airport tarmac, plus the problems of having to dodge a military guard. About the only thing that could drag Burak up on to the deck would be a pressing need to leave his haven in a great hurry.

Inside the ship is a different matter. Moving around in the command decks or the living quarters proves difficult. The interior is shoulder-to-shoulder, with people having to squeeze in the hallways to pass one another. Even the best practitioner of Obfuscate would have trouble making his way undetected. The hallway congestion of busy sailors running to and from duty posts, and the possibility of an alarm sending *everyone* running, mean that these cramped halls are another bad place to be.

The engineering compartments, therefore, are the place for a lurker to stay lost and out of sight. Miles of pipes carry everything from air conditioning to hydraulic fluids, engine fuel, special gases, weapons and ship sewage. It may not be possible to crawl *into* these pipes, but most of them are large enough to crawl *on*. (Crawling inside wouldn't be an especially pleasant experience, and it would be a lot harder to hide afterward with the smell of what those pipes carry clinging to one's clothes, hair and skin.) Since the engineering compartments place these pipes overhead, one can find a veritable forest of tubes to scurry along. Climbing and sliding turn it into a three-dimensional maze. With a little Potence, it's even possible to get into the insulation compartments of some bulkheads or into access corridors for damage control. All of these options offer hiding places into which people rarely go except in emergencies, and into which hardly anybody would think to look.

Burak sleeps in areas scattered throughout ceiling crawlways above several engine room halls. Since he must be able to move about the ship, he maintains several such spaces. As an ascetic he keeps few luxuries or personal items. He dares not risk keeping stored blood, because too much chance exists that it will be found or will fall out of a compartment and raise suspicions. His one concession to materialism is his prayer mat, a worn rug that he rolls up and carries in a small standard-issue military duffel bag (which draws no attention at all when he's Obfuscated to seem like just another crewman).

Luxuries

Even officers on naval vessels don't have many luxuries. There's enough room and supplies onboard for the crew to survive for an extended trip, but it doesn't have to be comfortable. News is sometimes piped through the ship on broadcast channels, and at least it's air-conditioned so that crews don't suffocate below decks. Other than that, everything else is milspec: tiny bathrooms (you have to duck to sit down), communal showers, bunk beds, mess hall. Decorations are frowned upon. Walls remain regulation gray. The sameness is almost enough to drive one crazy — especially since it's too risky to head upstairs at night except with *extreme* caution. Even then, though, there's nowhere to go.

Using an aircraft carrier as a haven does have one significant luxury as far as Kindred are concerned, however. It's impressive — even legendary. Many Kindred would scoff at the notion, considering it impossible to even get aboard, much less make a home for oneself there. But the thought of a Kindred secretly skulking about, perhaps influencing the crew's decisions, maybe even with a cloaked finger surreptitiously near a control for weapons… or for the ship's nuclear reactor… that's the sort of unpleasantness that sticks in the mind. Showing up at an Elysium while the ship is in port might draw uncomfortable laughs and some ridicule at first, but who *really* wants to find out if you actually have nuclear influence?

For Burak's purposes, of course, the ship's military arsenal is simply a deterrent. His real treasure lies in the ability to surround himself with the masses of humanity, yet remain safely hidden away. He has no need to deal with other Kindred, and he can practice his ascetic discipline freely. Indeed, only that tight discipline keeps him from making a fatal error. Every night he survives is testament to his iron self-control — and, in his mind, a minute step closer to salvation.

Feeding

Strict discipline is the order of the night for any Kindred moving with the military. If even one sailor turns up dead, a massive manhunt is sure to follow, along with a ship-wide investigation. This means that only *great* care allows Burak to pick out a rotating schedule of sailors for feeding. Working as a Sandman (i.e., feeding only from sailors who are on a sleeping shift and moving through the ship under cover of Obfuscate) is Burak's method of choice. Because most of the crew must bunk in communal rooms, though, even this practice is dangerous and prone to detection if Burak should fail to exercise caution. It is possible to catch the occasional lone engineer in a faraway compartment with the help of Dominate, but tampering with memory isn't always totally reliable.

It's also important to keep a rotating schedule of victims. A sailor who shows up in sick bay too often, or who goes for a physical and comes up with low blood pressure, may flag too much curiosity. Furthermore, Burak doesn't even try for the officers. While many of them have their own quarters, they also have more guards and will draw more suspicion if they show up for duty dizzy, lethargic and low on blood.

The occasional small vermin is almost an inevitable part of a ship's complement, especially in the World of Darkness. While the *Nimitz*-class carriers are especially scrubbed and cleaned, there's always room for something small and innocuous to hide. After all, if a vampire can hide himself away among the crew, a few rats can stow away easily. As long as the bodies make it into the trash chute or are flushed into the bilges, nobody's any the wiser when Burak eases his appetite with the occasional rat. True, rat blood is hardly nourishing or tasty to Kindred, but it's at least a passable supplement.

Fortunately, aircraft carriers at sea travel with escort vessels, which occasionally bring over new crew or exchange crew. In port, sailors go off-ship and maintenance workers come on board. Both of these times provide opportunities to find new vessels. While at dock, it's even possible to sneak out for a bite to eat and a run around town. Carriers of the *Carl Vinson*'s size can expect to spend a month in dry-dock for maintenance and upgrades, and when a scheduled refit comes around, this period can easily stretch up to six months.

Difficulties

The difficulties of making a haven in such a strange place are many and varied. Shifts of soldiers rotate on and off the ship regularly. The potential for a military alert could blow away the Masquerade. The cramped quarters allow barely any moving room. The occupant must spend six months in a claustrophobic maze of tubes, and he has virtually no escape if anything goes wrong. With a single misstep, the entire haven could become a death trap.

Therefore, only the strictest emotional discipline allows Burak to maintain his façade. Careful self-control keeps frenzy at bay when he is hungry, and rigorous attention to detail makes sure that he changes his sleeping area and stays out of places where maintenance crews are working. By pretending to be a crewman, he can move about the lower decks with at least some autonomy, especially if he seems to be "under orders" from someone already. The trick is to keep moving and look like he's already busy doing a job.

Of course, an aircraft carrier has another large potential problem — it's a military vessel. If any sort of military action comes up, it's on the front line. No place in a ship is 100-percent secure in that event. Torpedoes and high-caliber slugs don't just "miss" certain compartments, after all. Anything could explode, collapse or suddenly be flooded if an all-out battle takes place, and if Burak happens to be in a compromised compartment, he's in for a world of trouble. But at least a disfigured corpse isn't likely to draw excessive notice while sailors are working damage control.

The greatest challenge of the environment, though, is the constant struggle to maintain sanity. There are no other Kindred here, and Burak has no way to contact the outside world. No human can be trusted. A blood bond is terribly risky, if not outright impossible. If a thrall starts acting strangely, his behavior risks raising too many suspicions. Obfuscation may be able to disguise an inhuman appearance, but it can't disguise the fact that a Kindred doesn't have identification papers or a uniform, unless he steals one from the laundry — and even that has to go back before it's accounted missing. There's nobody to talk to, no one to deal with… Burak is surrounded by thousands of people but desperately alone. True, by using the Obfuscate Discipline, he can make the occasional foray out among the humans who surround him, but he doesn't eat, he can't risk being ordered above decks or brought under the scrutiny of an officer, and he must always worry that moving among humans risks a dangerous and final frenzy if the Hunger becomes a bit too much.

Only a supreme exercise of will allows Burak to maintain a hold on his sanity, because he knows that a single moment of frenzy will destroy this careful charade and cost him his haven. Loss of any control means being spotted, which means a by-the-book manhunt throughout the entire ship. Yet, keeping that handle on humanity becomes progressively more difficult since he has hardly any way to identify with anyone. Not only are the soldiers all numbered cogs in a military machine, they're his depersonalized victims. In such a situation, the erosion of humanity is almost inevitable.

About the only up side to the situation is that Burak has one nearly sure means of escape in the event of a catastrophic emergency, provided it occurs at night: diving into the ocean. As long as the pressure at depth is not too great and he knows which way to go, he can (uncomfortably) survive walking along and sleeping on a bottom shelf. If pressed, Burak could potentially steal a life raft and a body bag, but those *would* be noticed, and the Navy would track the raft's location transponder and send out a crew to recover it.

Maintenance

This type of haven demands no rent, no bills and no background checks, but even then, the price is high. The trick isn't so much maintaining a haven of this sort, as it is letting the haven maintain itself without getting caught. In some ways, it's a consummate exercise of the Masquerade, for nobody can so much as suspect anything. Even a single out-of-place leftover drop of blood or piece of clothing could bring the whole arrangement crashing in ruins.

Meanwhile, even the exercise of Disciplines is not always a sure thing. Sometimes, people remember things, even when memories are tampered with. Sailors have odd dreams and half-recognized, fleeting glimpses of hunched-over things below decks. Odd noises draw the occasional stare. Nobody among the officers would ever give such a thought credence, but a rumor of haunting could spread among the crew like a fad. Many might laugh it off or never take it seriously from the start, but others would cross themselves and go about their duties with military discipline, ever on the lookout for proof of what they fear. Nobody talks about it, but when the lights go to night shift and sailors head to their bunks, it creeps into the mind.

All it would take is one shred of potential proof.

Security

A nuclear-powered aircraft carrier has some of the most formidable defenses available to the modern military. Combine those with the carrier's stringent restrictions on personnel attendance and its long-term voyages at sea, and it's virtually the most secure haven one could imagine. It's so secure, in fact, that a single misstep by the inhabitant is disastrous.

Militarily, the *Carl Vinson* carries air search radars and surface search radars in multiple bands. Electronic warfare systems detect incoming enemy radar and determine scan type, providing an instant analysis of incoming craft, including what type they are, how many there are and what direction they're coming from. All of these systems provide intelligence for the carrier's weapons. For close defense, the ship carries six-barrel systems that fire 50 rounds per second up to a range of one mile. Chaff, sonar decoys and infrared flares work as countermeasures against incoming missiles and torpedoes. Short-range anti-missile systems are part of recent refits, and the full wings of reconnaissance and combat aircraft, which can launch at a rate of one jet per 20 seconds, provide long-range capabilities or close support. The hull is sheathed in two-and-a-half-inch thick armor plating, with redundant systems for emergencies and extra Kevlar layering over the engines and ammunition compartments. That's not even counting the escort vessels that typically accompany any carrier, bringing missile fire and heavy cannon support. Nobody's taking this baby in any sort of combat raid. Even the most crazed and deluded Sabbat shovelhead probably wouldn't consider it.

Since an aircraft carrier spends months at sea, it's a domain nearly inaccessible to other Kindred. There's no way for a typical Cainite to arrive except by special transfer from another military ship or as a civilian attaché on a transport aircraft. Very few Kindred have the influence to pull off that sort of business, and fewer still have the

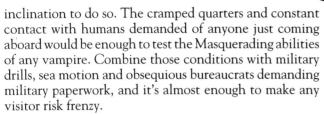

inclination to do so. The cramped quarters and constant contact with humans demanded of anyone just coming aboard would be enough to test the Masquerading abilities of any vampire. Combine those conditions with military drills, sea motion and obsequious bureaucrats demanding military paperwork, and it's almost enough to make any visitor risk frenzy.

In port, transfers of personnel are fairly routine. Still, the Navy doesn't risk having stowaways or potential crazies just wander in. Coming on board means having the proper ID and passing the guards on duty at the base, and maybe even at specific points in the ship. Even if someone gets on board, entering restricted areas means bypassing more armed guards. Only bringing to bear a *lot* of influence, or hefty uses of mind-altering Disciplines, can do that. For a vampire with superlative obfuscation capabilities, that's not much of a problem. For other Kindred, it's a chore.

Burak, for his part, stole aboard the vessel during part of its maintenance routine in the evening. Thanks to his obfuscatory talents, he could easily walk up the maintenance plank, looking like a contracted worker, and slip right into the engine room. Since the contractors take their roll calls in the morning *off* the ship, he never had to prove his identity against a checklist. Another group of Kindred might be able to sneak on board the same way, *if* they managed to get to a base while the ship was in dock and come aboard under similar pretenses (or with Dominate to back up faked "military authority").

Most importantly for the occupant, the close-in network of personnel combined with the need for proper military procedure and paperwork means that any new passengers aboard, especially non-military or unusual ones, will draw immediate attention. Burak will almost certainly learn of the arrival of other Kindred at once.

Future

The US Navy commissioned the *Carl Vinson* in 1982, but already all of the *Nimitz*-class carriers are undergoing refits. This means significant time in port, but it also means engineers and mechanics crawling through ducts or places otherwise left unused. Sometimes it means changing the layout of passages or maintenance corridors. In any event, it means Burak must get the hell out from under decks and keep moving to avoid detection. Overhauls happen in shipyards, though, rather than at sea, so at least it's possible to *walk* out under cover of Obfuscate. Of course, getting back on board afterward and learning how the layout of his haven has changed would then be a daunting proposition.

As military carriers age, even refits of technology can't always keep up. The navy — and the changes in policy toward smaller military forces — mean that the old carrier's day may soon come to an end. Eventually the USS *Carl Vinson* will have to be decommissioned, and then, it will be time for Burak to look for a new home.

Story Ideas

• With Ur-Shulgi's recent crackdown on the Assamite clan, Burak's disappearance comes under closer scrutiny than it was given when it occurred. The players' coterie is offered a boon in exchange for tracking him down and bringing him in for a consultation with his elders.

• While the *Carl Vinson* is on standard deployment, Burak accidentally kills someone on board. He manages to make the death look accidental, but there is a full naval inquest nonetheless. He manages to steal a radio long enough to send a cryptic message for help to a Nosferatu contact he made the last time he was on land. The coterie intercepts the message and must figure out what's going on, and then determine how to use its influence to stall paperwork at the nearest naval base long enough to kill the investigation.

• A coterie member seeking Golconda hears of a hidden ascetic who can show the way to live peacefully among humanity. The coterie seeks out Burak for his experience and knowledge.

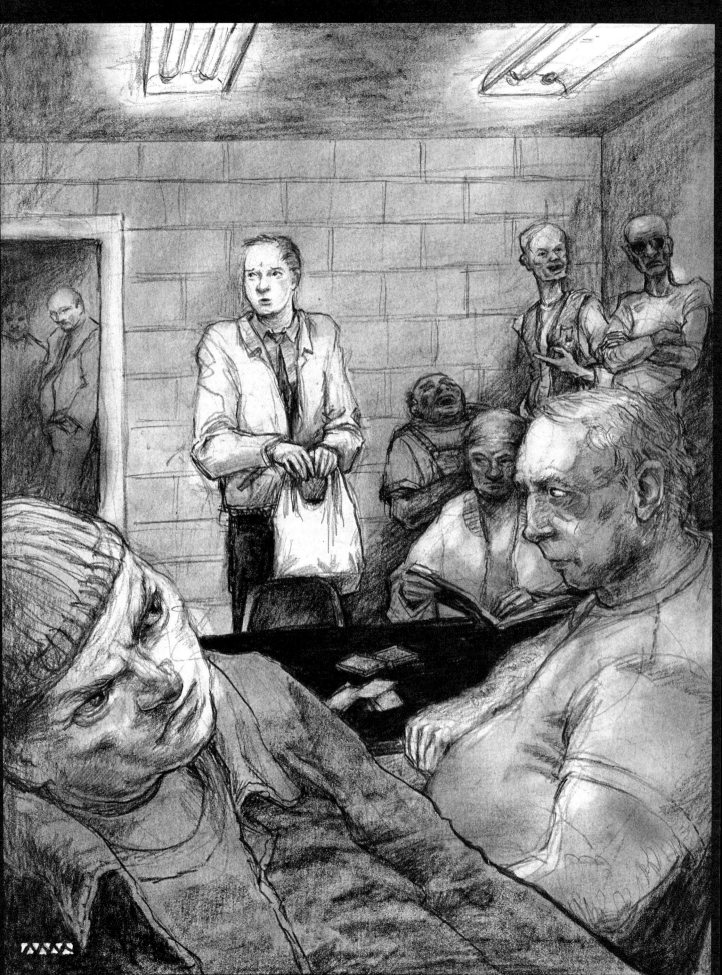

The Chattanooga Recreational Center

It is no secret among the undead that Cainites are social creatures who come together and congregate unobserved among humankind. Unlike a close-knit group of humans working toward a common goal, however, vampiric society tends to discourage any sort of camaraderie or fellowship among its Cainites that is not strictly self-serving or outright predatory. This sort of emotional bond is detrimental to a Cainite's security because it provides a pathway to potential weaknesses that a savvier (and less humane) vampire can exploit. It's true that Kindred cooperate for mutual protection, overpowering strength on the hunt or to solidify noncompetitive influences over the mortal world, but nothing is free in the Kindred world, and in the end, it's every vampire for himself.

This schizoid approach to teamwork requires immense mental fortitude and constant self-control. It also erodes the lingering vestiges of humanity that all Kindred must preserve against the depredations of the Beast. Human beings are social creatures as well, but on some level, humans crave and rely on a certain unquestioning trust in their interpersonal relationships. Lacking that fundamental underpinning, Cainites eventually succumb to insane paranoia or fall victim to those of their peers who know better than to put empty hope in trust.

Consider, then, the fate of an aging vampire who, in order to preserve his humanity (and lacking any other recourse) desires honest interaction that does not demand quid pro quo for every favor. What is this seeker to do? In the case of Doctor Phillip Andrews, the answer lies in the collection of down-and-outs who haunt the confines of the Chattanooga Recreational Center.

Resident

Like many unlucky men and women before him, Doctor Andrews knows what it's like to exist as a pariah in a society that ought to accept him. Before he was Embraced, he was a respected and fairly affluent doctor with a growing practice. He was unmarried, but he dated frequently and at his leisure, and he wasn't unhappy keeping to himself the rest of the time. His patients respected him, as did his colleagues.

The comfort and relative ease of his life fell apart, however, when he was stalked and attacked by an unknown assailant as he made his way home late one night from his office. In a blur of violence and sudden, unexpected, ecstasy, some vampire grabbed him, knocked him down and drained him dry. The vampire then Embraced

Doctor Andrews, but something went wrong. Instead of awaking immediately, Andrews remained in torpor, seemingly dead, for hours. No one knows how long his sire waited around, but he eventually lost hope and abandoned his aborted fledgling.

Doctor Andrews didn't awaken until near dawn. Although he was unaware of it in the frenzy that swiftly came upon him, he had been taken to a local hospital and pronounced dead, and an unlucky orderly had just wheeled him into the morgue to await his autopsy. In the vampiric cover-up that followed the next night, the mess that Doctor Andrews made was labeled a break-in resulting in murder and the theft of Doctor Andrews' corpse. The scourge of the domain tracked Andrews down roughly a week later and brought him before the bored local Kindred authorities.

Having come to his senses and remained horrified in hiding, Andrews tried to enlist the Kindred's aid in figuring out who had sired him and what he was supposed to do now. None of the locals, however, cared enough to help. His facility with the Presence and Auspex Disciplines suggested that he might be the castoff experiment of a local Toreador, but none of them admitted to creating him. His ability to use the rudiments of the Dominate Discipline suggested that he might be a Tremere progeny, but the local brood of Warlocks refused to even test his blood, and the prince didn't push the issue. Since no one came forward to take credit for Andrews' Embrace, he was deemed Caitiff and released to go about his business (after a brief warning about the Traditions and a promise that he would be summarily executed if he violated any of them).

Thereafter, Andrews quickly learned what it meant to be Caitiff in a Camarilla domain. No one would act or speak on his behalf unless he could offer them something directly in return, and he was too young and naïve a vampire to have anything to offer. On top of that, he wasn't streetwise enough to know how to get money or fake identification or to otherwise recoup any of the luxuries (or even basic amenities) he'd enjoyed while he was alive. Finally, in desperation, he swallowed the last of his pride and stumbled into the Chattanooga Recreational Center pretending to be a wandering bum who'd lost everything.

Those who roomed there, he found, were a dirty and downtrodden lot, ranging from simple vagrants and petty thieves to the Technicolor oddity of persons not sufficiently insane to warrant being institutionalized. Regardless of what made them unique, though, the residents were all very strict about keeping illegal activities outside of the building. Criminal acts such as selling or using drugs, stealing from each other or brutalizing one another would have meant a one-way ticket to the sidewalk, if not straight to jail. Plus, should a pattern of criminal acts develop in the shelter, the city could pull its funding, and then everyone would be left without a roof.

The small dose of civility enforced by this discretion had started to chip off the rough exterior of the residents, and it made an immediate impression on Andrews. The residents weren't Boy Scouts, to be sure, but the conditions imposed upon them in return for housing have created a rude sort of community among the tenants. While many of them are still petty and distasteful to the eyes of a higher-class observer, the tenants share what little they have with each other. Watching a scavenged TV in the multi-purpose room or sharing bed space with one another is a far cry from the sink-or-swim mentality of the streets. Dr. Andrews, in turn, has found the loose honesty among those who have nothing to lose to be a welcome refresher from the closed lips and hearts of the undead.

Appearance

The Rec Center is located on the outskirts of the downtown area, pressed up against the former industrial area on the south side of the river. As Chattanooga has grown, the urban trappings that the area's original inhabitants sought to escape have increasingly surrounded this former first line of suburbia. The first impression of the area for those visiting should be one of crushing *sameness*, with nearly identical houses and ill-kept yards butting up against fast food joints distinguishable only by the color-scheme of cheap uniform worn by the drones who operate the equipment. This part of town is a far cry from the "revitalization" projects currently going on near the Tennessee Aquarium in the heart of the city.

The building itself is a monument to cookie-cutter, poured-concrete modernism, in the style that was once called "modern" by the tasteless city planners of days gone by. The building is essentially a two-story block, with a gymnasium addition fused on to the rear without regard for aesthetic considerations. While the physical construction is sound, the layout leaves a great deal to be desired. This ignoble foundation is not helped by the lack of upkeep, a result of community donations dying off as those who could afford to be charitable pulled up stakes and moved on, heading either to the north side of the river or south across the Georgia border. The working-class poor who took their place have neither the time nor the money to help the Rec Center maintain itself, although they rely greatly on the beleaguered staff for things such as after-school care and athletic clubs for their children.

Until recently, the staff comprised mainly volunteers, some of whom were former residents of the shelter. Some small improvements have been made to the building, under the direction of Terrell Buell, the center's director (such as replacing a water heater that barely survived the Carter administration and replacing all of the gymnasium's broken windows), but lack of funding has been a persistent problem. Desperate for cash, the Rec Center has begun providing rooms for the homeless and other drifters in order to receive funds through a city-grant program. Rooms for the men have been created on the second floor of the main building.

LAYOUT

Staff offices and the internal controls for the heating and cooling system, as well as three multi-purpose rooms, take up most of the first floor. The multi-purpose rooms are in the style so popular in public architecture, combining the dismal decoration of fluorescent lighting and green tile with the stultifying sameness of folding chairs and tables bought in bulk. At the end of the main hallway, a set of double doors leads into the gymnasium, which comprises a (barely) regulation basketball court and a collection of worn-out dumbbells. The court area is dimly lit, with paint peeling off the bleachers and upper sections of the walls. The odor of 40 years of sweat has accumulated in the atmosphere, and those who attend the occasional pickup basketball game have dubbed the room the "gym sock" by way of description.

The second floor holds the living areas for most of the Rec Center's tenants. Only slightly larger than the first-floor closet occupied by Doctor Andrews, these are poor excuses for living quarters. Each room holds one thread-bare cot, a small and long-suffering wooden chest of drawers (many of which are pitted by graffiti and cigarette burns), and one or two of the dozens of straight-back chairs procured during some long-ago program of summer arts-and-crafts classes. The floors are gritty tile grids covered in cheap area rugs purchased in bulk in Dalton, Georgia, and the walls are painted cinderblock. These have been re-painted so often that deep nicks and gouges often reveal several layers of color without exposing the gray material beneath. Most are also streaked from dirty human fingers or dingy from the tenants smoking in their chairs next to their windows.

The men who dwell here may personalize their rooms to some extent, but given their lack of resources and the frequent turnover of tenants, the rooms tend to remain in their original condition. A paint touchup and a porcelain Nativity scene bought at the Salvation Army sale brighten one old gentleman's room upstairs, and some of the other long-time residents have begun to follow his example.

Mr. Buell has taken note of this welcome brightening of the mood, and he is encouraging its development by increasing the number of group activities the Rec Center hosts. Doctor Andrews has latched on to the rise in collective action, speaking privately with the director about activities suggested by the staff. The staff is beginning to seek his opinion more often as well, as they come to appreciate his surprisingly educated opinions on how to support the developing camaraderie.

The room Doctor Andrews keeps is the only such room on the first floor of the Rec Center. In keeping with the rest of the building, it is thoroughly depressing from an architectural standpoint, and the bed and dresser are even closer together than those in the upstairs chambers. The door is the only means of exit, as there is no window or vent leading to the outside. The room was once a storage closet next to the fire exit on the left of the building, converted into a residence at the insistence of a poor man in a wheelchair who formerly occupied it. That man died before Doctor Andrews showed up, so securing the room for himself was only a matter of issuing a few Dominate commands and backing them up with the Entrancement power of Presence.

When the doctor is in the room, the only open space is the small area between the bed and dresser. The place doesn't have a chair to sit in. The previous tenant had just enough room to roll his wheelchair in and back out again, but not to turn it around. Even now, the room is small and shabby, its size a mirror of its occupant's dwindling ego and hope. Dr. Andrews has barely begun to care enough about the shelter to decorate his living space, and the room serves as a barometer for the redevelopment of his soul. What little money he makes working crappy night jobs in the city has gone into buying a few changes of second-hand clothes, used paperback novels (by Robin Cook, James Patterson and Dean Koontz), generic toiletries, a one-foot-square mirror for his door and a battery-powered reading lamp.

The rest of the decorations in the small space are personal odds and ends he's hung onto that remind him of what it was to be human. They include an empty single-serving scotch bottle minus the label that he found in the grass outside, an unopened paper pack of Marlboro menthols that the room's previous tenant left under the bed, a matte-black Zippo lighter that an upstairs neighbor gave him, a month-old stack of newspapers and TV guides, and a ticket stub for the movie *Rudy* (a souvenir from one Christmas when the director took the locals out to a fast-food dinner and a show at the dollar theater). He also bought and keeps a well-stocked Johnson & Johnson first-aid kit on his dresser, and he has encouraged his fellow residents to come to him when they have minor injuries that need tending. Although even the most long-time residents know nothing about his life before he came to the Rec Center, all of the regulars have taken to calling him Doctor Andrews as a joke.

SECURITY

Having been scorned by the area's better-established Kindred, Doctor Andrews is very concerned with keeping his retreat secret from them. Despite his lack of any real influence over it and his inability to defend it should some other vampire come around causing trouble, he considers the place his own. The first thing he realized when he discovered this haven was that he had to keep from drawing the attention of other Kindred to it. Therefore, the most important action he takes to keep his new home secret is no overt action at all. He hasn't gone looking for any Kindred contacts, and he has more or less given up trying to find out who his sire was (although the mystery still bothers him).

As for keeping secret what he is within the shelter, he has taken advantage of the de facto segregation that staying downstairs and working only at night provides. The separate living quarters gives him privacy when he needs it, while keeping him close to the ebb and flow of the small society formed by the other residents. He talks to them in the common rooms before he leaves "for work," he shows up to watch all the evening pickup basketball games, and he attends the occasional sponsored group outing after dark, but he spends most of his time in his room with the door locked. Therefore, the fact that he doesn't come out of his room during the day and hardly ever answers when people knock doesn't seem especially strange.

The doctor also uses his Discipline powers to help keep his secret. Every few months, he makes the rounds of the staff and longer-term tenants to cloud their memories about just how long he's been downstairs in the room by the fire exit. They all know he's been a resident "for years," but beyond that, they can't say with certainty. His rare use of Entrancement keeps newcomers and stronger-willed regulars from getting dangerously suspicious. The frequent turnover of rootless drifters and welfare cases who get back on their feet quickly aids Doctor Andrews in this effort as well.

Where feeding is concerned, Doctor Andrews plays a dangerous game of strict self-control and constant shepherding of memory. Once a week, he steals into the other tenants' rooms while they're asleep, drinks a small draught of vitae from each of them, then commands them to forget the experience and go back to sleep. He then tops off on whatever rats (or the occasional stray dog or cat) he can catch and dispose of on the Rec Center grounds. Having never been taught to hunt properly, he has never been told how dangerous hunting in the same building where he sleeps (even hunting as a Sandman or preying on animals) can be. He has not yet lost control of himself, though, so his secret is safe as far as he can tell.

Uncovering Doctor Andrews

Doctor Andrews' security strategy is based around inaction, so the easiest way for him to be exposed is if he must take steps that he has not anticipated. For example, the Rec Center has not needed a major repair in some time, but should some expense arise (the furnace breaks down irreparably in the dead of winter, or a water main bursts), the Center does not have the ready funds to correct such a problem. Such a situation would require Doctor Andrews to assist in some way or else watch his refuge get shuttered, since state or local authorities would likely be unwilling to foot the bill. Because he has few personal assets and no pull within the local community, Doctor Andrews might, in desperation, seek out one of the local Kindred and beg for assistance.

Story Ideas

• Looking for a quick spot to grab a bite and crash, a nomadic gang of anarchs (i.e., the players' characters) stops in at the Rec Center. They're about to move on, but they discover Doctor Andrews while he's up hunting one night. They must decide whether they should simply leave him alone (which could prove a liability later on if they intend to cause trouble without getting caught) or if they should try to convince him to join them in their quest for vampiric equality. The doctor would prefer the former, but would not be averse to the latter if the characters make the unlifestyle of the Anarch Movement sound good enough.

• An older, more powerful Kindred decides coincidentally to use the Rec Center as a backup haven on those nights when hunting takes her too far from her primary haven. Amused to find Doctor Andrews there, she summarily ousts him, driving him back into the city desperate for shelter. Outraged and panicked, the doctor runs into one or more members of the coterie, who happen to be bitter rivals of the more powerful Kindred. In return for kicking the rival Kindred back out so that Doctor Andrews can return home, the doctor offers to tell the coterie exactly where to find the usurper and how to get to her without raising the suspicions of the Rec Center staff or its current residents.

• On a whim, the local prince's scourge decides to find out who the doctor's sire is. He sends mortal agents during the day to collect a blood sample, then has the coterie take it to an ally of his in a chantry out of town to test it thaumaturgically. The answer turns out to be a surprise, and if word of it gets out, it could seriously destabilize the sire's base of power in the city. (Perhaps Doctor Andrews was privy to some important information before his death, and his sire Embraced him hoping to secure control over it.) Depending on the political dynamic of the chronicle, the coterie might then need to get to the doctor, find out what he knows and keep him safe from his sire's henchmen. Alternatively, they might need to get to the doctor on his sire's behalf and eliminate him before his sire's secret gets out.

Coming Soon...
World of Darkness Mafia

year of the Damned

main books

VAMPIRE: THE MASQUERADE
WW2300
$29.95 U.S.

The core rulebook for the game of modern horror. Hardcover.

GUIDE TO THE CAMARILLA
WW2302
$25.95 U.S.

The core resource on the foremost sect of vampires. Hardcover.

GUIDE TO THE SABBAT
WW2303
$25.95 U.S.

The core resource on the Camarilla's undead rivals. Hardcover.

clanbooks

Clanbooks contain vital character information for players and Storytellers.

CLANBOOK: ASSAMITE WW2359 $14.95 U.S.	**CLANBOOK: GIOVANNI** WW2363 $14.95 U.S.	**CLANBOOK: TOREADOR** WW2356 $14.95 U.S.
CLANBOOK: BRUJAH WW2351 $14.95 U.S.	**CLANBOOK: LASOMBRA** WW2362 $14.95 U.S.	**CLANBOOK: TREMERE** WW2357 $14.95 U.S.
CLANBOOK: FOLLOWERS OF SET WW2360 $14.95 U.S.	**CLANBOOK: MALKAVIAN** WW2353 $14.95 U.S.	**CLANBOOK: TZIMISCE** WW2361 $14.95 U.S.
CLANBOOK: GANGREL WW2352 $14.95 U.S.	**CLANBOOK: NOSFERATU** WW2354 $14.95 U.S.	**CLANBOOK: VENTRUE** WW2358 $14.95 U.S.
	CLANBOOK: RAVNOS WW2364 $14.95 U.S.	

other supplements

ART OF VAMPIRE: THE MASQUERADE
WW2298 $14.95 U.S.
The lavishly illustrated art book that accompanied the Vampire limited edition now available individually.

BLOOD MAGIC: SECRETS OF THAUMATURGY
WW2106 $19.95 U.S.
A long-awaited resource that contains the most jealously guarded powers of blood magicians.

BOOK OF NOD
WW2251 $10.95 U.S.
The tome of vampires' proposed origins and history. Tradeback.

CAIRO BY NIGHT
WW2410 $15.95 U.S.

chicago chronicles volume 2
WW2235 $20.00 U.S.
Combines Chicago by Night Second Edition and Under a Blood Red Moon

CHILDREN OF THE NIGHT
WW2023 $14.95 U.S.
The masters of the undead in the Final Nights.

CITIES OF DARKNESS VOLUME 3
WW2624 $16.00 U.S.
Combines Alien Hunger and Dark Colony

DIRTY SECRETS OF THE BLACK HAND
WW2006 $18.00 U.S.
Secret rules and powers for this hidden sect.

ETERNAL HEARTS
WW2400 $19.95 U.S.
A novella from Black Dog Game Factory that examines the vampire as a sexual metaphor. For adults only.

GHOULS: FATAL ADDICTION
WW2021 $15.00 U.S.
The guide to playing vampires' human pawns.

THE GILDED CAGE
WW2420 $15.95 U.S.

GIOVANNI CHRONICLES IV: NUOVA MALATTIA
WW2097 $19.95 U.S.
For adults only.

THE GIOVANNI SAGA I
WW2098 $17.95 U.S.
The epic adventure of undead betrayal and power across the ages. Contains parts I and II of the Giovanni Chronicles. For adults only.

MIDNIGHT SIEGE
WW2422 $19.95 U.S.

NEW YORK BY NIGHT
WW2411 $17.95 U.S.

NIGHTS OF PROPHECY
WW2265 $19.95 U.S.
Secrets revealed and cycles turned in the Year of Revelations.

REVELATIONS OF THE DARK MOTHER
WW2024 $10.95 U.S.
New insight into vampire origins and the undead curse itself, in the Book of Nod tradition. Tradeback.

SINS OF THE BLOOD
WW2421 $17.95 U.S.

THE TIME OF THIN BLOOD
WW2101 $15.95 U.S.
Allows you to portray the hunted childer of high-generation vampires.

VAMPIRE STORYTELLERS COMPANION
WW2301 $14.95 U.S.
The essential screen and resource book for Vampire Storytellers.

VAMPIRE STORYTELLERS HANDBOOK (REVISED EDITION)
WW2304 $25.95 U.S.
The core reference for Vampire Storytellers. Hardcover.

for more information visit us online:
www.white-wolf.com

VAMPIRE
THE MASQUERADE

World of Darkness: Mafia™

The Possessed Players Guide™ for Werewolf: The Apocalypse™

Heresies of the Way™ for Kindred of the East™

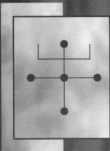

Hunter: Fall from Grace™ for Hunter: The Reckoning®

Year of the Damned

What is the Price of Power? Money? Service? Your eternal soul?

The Year of the Damned explores the lengths to which the denizens of the World of Darkness are prepared to go to fulfill their lofty ideals and foul cravings. Does the end justify the means? Can any worldly reward be worthwhile when the Devil demands his due?

2002 is the Year of the Damned. Secretive deals are sealed, ominous pacts are broken and dark forces descend upon the Earth. Can the World of Darkness pay the ultimate price? Delve into the following books to find out!

Dark Ages: Inquisitor™ for Dark Ages: Vampire™

State of Grace™ for Vampire: The Masquerade®

Demon: The Fallen™

©2002. White Wolf is a registered trademark of White Wolf Publishing, Inc. All trademarks are owned by White Wolf Publishing Inc. All rights reserved.